Say My Name

the memoirs of Charlie Louie

Say My Name

the memoirs of Charlie Louie

Linda Rogers

Ekstasis Editions

Canadian Cataloguing in Publication Data

Rogers, Linda
    Say my name.

        Novel
        ISBN 1-896860-78-8

                I. Title.
        PS8585.O392S3   2000   C813'.54   C00-911090-9
        PR9199.2.R634S3   2000

Published in 2000 by:
Ekstasis Editions Canada Ltd.   Ekstasis Editions
Box 8474, Main Postal Outlet   Box 571
Victoria, B.C. V8W 3S1   Banff, Alberta T0L 0C0

THE CANADA COUNCIL | LE CONSEIL DES ARTS
FOR THE ARTS | DU CANADA
SINCE 1957 | DEPUIS 1957

Say My Name has been published with the assistance of a grant from the Canada Council and the Cultural Services Branch of British Columbia.

for Sasha, Keefer and Tristan, and for our brother C.

and bill, who is wiser than anyone knows, even him

Foreword

In the early seventies, I moved with my young family to a sheep farm in the Cowichan Valley. Our next door neighbours were the families living on the Number 11 Reserve. Even their home had no name. These people became our friends. One elder taught me to make cedar root baskets and another to spin and knit wool. We fished and gathered berries together.

I established a library and fine arts program at a local parochial school that was partly funded by the Department of Indian Affairs and had Cowichan elders participating in language and craft programs for the children. One boy became precious to me. He lost his parents when he was still in infancy, and, because of aboriginal policy about adopting out of First Nations families, we could not think of legally bringing him into our own.

He was left in the care of older siblings struggling to raise their own young children, but his real parent was the wind. Our boy loved to run. It didn't matter where.

"Charlie" remained a cherished member of our extended family, taking part in farm life, haying and riding, and he especially loved puppet shows and dressing up, painting and working with clay. We had a special bond. I lost a son in childbirth about the same time his parents died, one of exposure and the other by choking, the grim effects of alcoholism, fallout from the cruelty of residential schools.

He grew up and left school as so many First Nations children do when they feel invisible in our educational system. In late adolescence, this loving gentle youth began to act out because he had reason to. He ended up, like so many young native boys who have been neglected, marginalized and abused, in jail.

We moved to the city and news travelled more slowly. One Christmas, we were diverted by a highway accident, taking the Brentwood ferry back to Saanich and Victoria. The overloaded car in front of us was having a problem with a trunk that kept flying open. It was a situation straight out of vaudeville. Finally, the driver, a big man, got out and gave it a hard slam. By then, we were all laughing.

When the driver came over to greet us, I realized he was Slater Bob, a boy I had known, who was now a recovered alcoholic and Pentecostal preacher. I immediately asked Slater about "our child", wondering why we hadn't heard from him. His eyes changed and, in the time he was trying to frame a palatable answer because First Nations people do not like to bring bad news, I knew.

Our boy had followed several of his brothers and sisters into the woods, where they took turns taking the family shot-gun and turning it on themselves. More often than not, this ended in something short of physical death, another failure. A family portrait would show people with different parts of their face or brain missing. "Charlie" had succeeded.

Because we had missed the initial grieving process, my children and I thought about a fitting memorial. We planted a tree, but it was not enough. There are so many like him in this land of plenty that does not take care of its children, I felt I had to tell his story in my own way.

The following book is fiction, but the details are true. It is my story and his, but I chose to tell it in his voice, because it is one that I know so well. An animal mother recognizes the sound her own baby makes. That is how they find one another. This story is my attempt to find our boy and share him with you, so that you might better understand what it is like to be a boy like him.

Our son and brother was a good and valuable person, full of talent and compassion. However, he had one freedom and that was to choose another world should he wish to, and he did, knowing that his parents and grandparents were already there. This story, although sad, is a record of his many kindnesses and wonderful sense of humour, much of which revealed the ironies in non-Indian behaviour.

I would like to thank all those who have encouraged me to tell this story; my husband and children, Chief Tony Hunt, whose niece is doing her doctorate in the area of youth suicide among aboriginal people, Chief Lindsay Marshall, who lost a family member, elder Norm Harry, a vocal victim of the residential school system, bill bissett, Stephen Reid, who has walked the walk, Al Purdy, who told me just before he died that this was my most important poem, Vera Wabegijig, beloved student and fresh young voice in the new poetry, Ian Johnstone, who told me how much this story helped him get through the grief for a young Indian suicide who had been in his care, Angela Addison, who pushed her failing eyesight to read it and offer comment, to Rick Van Krugal, to Douglas Henderson and Barbara Colebrook Peace, my ever wise and thoughtful editor.

Special thanks to Ekstasis Press, who published this difficult book, because they have the altruism to stand behind their intention to make the world a better place for our children.

Linda Rogers, Victoria, June 2000

1.
My Real Family

You never know where a baby came from. I seen babies that came out of dumpsters and some that got found in the trees. Lots of them get mixed up in the hospital. You can tell. There are all these kids that don't look like their parents, like my sister Rose's baby. Rose had this stomach ache and she didn't want to mess with Indian medicine, so Bernadette from the band office took her to the hospital in a taxi. Rose is a big girl and nobody knew she was pregnant, not even her. We all thought the white doctor was going to cut something bad out of her but when she came back she had this baby and it had black curly hairs.

Indians don't have black curly hairs. Indian hairs are long and straight. Rose must of got the wrong baby or maybe they just gave her one to take home because they felt sorry for her.

Rose loved this baby and she kept her real clean and nice. She washed her stuff every day with lots of bleach. Everything on the clothesline she rigged up from our front porch to the big cedar tree was white. The baby got whiter too. Its hairs turned orange and its skin looked like it had snow all over it.

When I held the baby, it didn't smell like a baby. It smelled like one of them school toilets. People started talking about this brown baby that was turning into a white baby and complaining about the smell.

Pret'soon the welfare people came and took the baby and Rose went crazy. She was starting up big bonfires and scrubbing our front steps with a brush. Rose was cleaning all night and all day and she kept one eye open for the taxi to bring her daughter back but they never and now Rose is not right in the head. The welfare people told us the baby got given to a white family that wouldn't of taken it in the first place when it was brown. So they should of thanked Rose for their white baby, but they never did.

My mother was called Angela like them angels and she died when I was a baby. It happened one night when she and my dad were out drinking and she couldn't get out of the car so my dad left her there. It was winter time and it was real cold. I was asleep in her arms, wrapped up tight in a blanket. Maybe because he knew in his heart that I didn't belong to him, my father forgot about me when he left her there all by herself.

The next morning, my mum was dead and I was alive, bawling for milk, I guess. My dad was sleeping it off but my big sister heard and she opened the car door and there I was. Sister Mary Joseph showed me this picture of Mary with Jesus in her arms only it was the opposite to me. In her picture, Jesus was the dead one.

I never got to ask my mum if I was in the right family, but I guess I wasn't. Not one hundred percent. I got this one blue eye. Sister told me the priests would of burned me at the stake in the olden days on account of two different coloured eyes meant you had the devil spirit in you.

I never thought too much of priests, especially after Father Jim, so I never believed that story.

My real father was white and I know who he is on account of a lot of things, starting with my blue eye and that dream I had. The next thing is the bleeding. I used to get this holy thing in my hands. They bled and they wouldn't stop and Sister said it was a sign from God that I came from a chief's family. And then there is this other problem which is like in that fairy tale she told me. I can't stand for certain things to touch me, like the labels on clothes.

Sister Mary Joseph said I was high strung and high strung people have extra nerve endings, so she got me old clothes that were broke in and she cut the labels out because I was wearing things inside out and the kids made fun of me. She said pay no attention anyway, because inside out was good luck.

I was the only one just about all the boys picked on, the Indian kids and the honky kids. None too many of them people at that school wanted to be my friend. Just Sister and Star and Mayzelle and my farm brothers who no one would play with 'cause they were hippies that played music. Sister said to keep it a secret but she loved me the best of all the kids in the school which was over two hundred, so that's pret'good, in'it?

She said my dream might of been true and I could be the son of a chief with blue eyes and she read me this story about a princess who went crazy over a pea in her bed. It was her who got me going about my true family because I saw my real father in a picture book she showed me from before I was born and he matched the guy I dreamed about.

Sister got asked to be a Indian and she had her own song and everything. They took her in the bear clan and it was real funny watching her dance because she taught the girls at school to do this dancing from her old country. Her Indian dancing was kind of like that too and it made the elders laugh because she picked her feet up in the air like a horse in the snow.

13

Sister took pictures with a camera and put them in these scrapbooks. There was pictures of every kid she ever taught and pictures of nuns on holidays and pictures of my people and big dances even though you're not supposed to, including the time the Queen came with her husband and the one of her kids that I think is my real father. The elders gave the Queen family Indian names and taught her son a chief's dance. He was the prince of whales from the whale clan. There is a picture of him and he has blue eyes that look right at you.

I think he was looking at my pret'mother dancing around the fire and that is how she got to kiss a prince even though Sister Mary Joseph told me you can kiss a prince and he can turn into a frog. She said nuns know about that kind of thing and that is why they are nuns because Jesus is a prince who only changes into a lamb. Anyway, that's where I got the idea for my scrapbook, which I kept for a long time until that white guy made fun of me in the bar that night. Then I burned it.

I heard my real father is coming to visit and I know this lady who told me I can catch a ride to go see him. I hope him and my little brothers like me.

2.
How I Got Angelina's Knife

I always thought fog was clouds that came close to the ground. If you could find the right one, you could lie down on it and it would be soft, but you wouldn't fall through it. If I ever went up in a airplane, I would see all these people sitting on air and lying down on it. They would be saints and angels and people I knew and they would be playing songs like the ones they sing at church. My mother would be waiting there. She would be sober and all dressed up in a white dress that never got dirty from kids climbing all over her. She would be keeping an eye out for me.

In one dream, I was flying the airplane and I had a long white scarf. My mother was waving at me when I went by with my white scarf flying in the wind. She looked like my sister LaVerne who has green eyes like the mud in the river. I woke up before I got close enough to touch my mother.

At school, Sister Mary Joseph made us sit on the magic carpet for story time. We could go anywhere we wanted. She took us to beautiful places with high mountains and flowers that grow in the snow. When she let me have a turn, I always chose Heaven so

I could see my mother. Sister said the clouds were magic carpets too and they carried the dead people around so they could look down on the people they left behind.

When I do a bad thing, I look up to see if there is any clouds in case my mother is watching. I am more scared of her seeing me and thinking I am bad than people down here finding out about it. Down here, they can give me a detention or take me to the Bighouse or jail to punish me but that is not so bad. The worse thing would be my mother not wanting me there when it was my time to go to spirit in case I gave her family a bad name.

It is hard to remember my dad. He smelled like liquor and that stuff he put on his hair to make it lie down. Even when I was a real little kid and hardly walking, he took me down to the river with the big kids. "You got to know the river," he said. My dad said the river was his church. He wasn't into praying, and the truth is, he never said much of anything. He could stand by that river, still as a tree, all day long, looking into the water, staring down those big fish that didn't much want to end up in our smokehouse.

When my dad got himself a big dog salmon full of eggs, he was respectful and he thanked her for getting caught so we could have food to eat.

In the summer, we went to the river by ourselves and we could splash all we liked, but my dad learned me and my brothers and sisters to be quiet as leaves at the time when the dogs come up the river to lay their eggs. I came out of my late mother at that time and the Indian name I was going to get but din't because we never got the money for my dance is Xwixelanew, which means the leaf that falls when the dogs are running.

I landed on ground that was far away from both my family trees, but I get to remember one and I seen pictures of the castle where my real father lives. The whole family sleeps together there, just like Indians, but they got their own rooms and their own beds.

16

When my dad was alive, he was the only one with his own bed in our family. I slept with Lester who gave me cooties and Wally and Cecile and their kids had two beds in one room and all three of my big sisters slept in the bed we got from Sister Evangelina, the fat nun that died.

Every night my sisters fought about who got to sleep where. None of them wanted to be in the middle because the bed was broke there and the other two girls rolled on top of you in the middle of the night. Besides, Angie cried herself to sleep all the time and LaVerne snored, especially after that boyfriend from Duncan broke her nose.

When my dad went off partying down at the jungle with Sam and them, Angelina climbed in his bed, that used to be my late mother's bed too, so she could sleep close to her. She said the ghost of my mother was in that bed and I wanted to get in too but Angelina wouldn't let me. She sure could kick hard.

There was this one night that started with a real nice dinner. It was stew with deer meat and lots of potatoes in it and bread and dessert because my late dad went to town to cash the welfare cheque and he came back in the taxi with ice cream and those marshmallow cookies with the pink coconut on them. Then my dad went out drinking with Sam and them on account of they still had their money.

I sat on the couch and watched wrestling with my brothers. They let me stay up special because our dad was out. Our dad always made the little kids go to bed. I slept on the sofa that night. I don't think I even lay down. Angie got into our dad's bed in the corner of that room with the sofa and the T.V.

When our dad came back the T.V. was still on but us kids was all asleep. I heard him get into bed with Angie. I heard her tell him to get off and I heard her roll him over on his back which is not the way he went to sleep.

In the morning, Angie must of got back in her own bed and our dad was still lying on his back and he was alone. I needed to use the outhouse and I was scared to go by myself, because there was cougars and bears out there, so I tried to wake our dad up, but he didn't. He was real cold and the hairs on my arms stood up straight because I remembered that from before. I always get cold when I think of my mother and her arms around me so tight they had to pull me out of them, which makes me think she meant to take me with her and I could of been one of those baby angels they have around at Christmas time.

I have to admit I got mad at my father and I punched him and yelled at him, but he didn't wake up, even though his eyes were wide open.

They said he choked in the night. He shouldn't of been lying on his back like that. It made him swallow his throw-up. That made me a paper orphan. There was no going back on that.

Angelina gave me her carving knife with the eagle on it and told me the knife would cut me bad if I ever told anyone she was the one that did it. If she hadn't rolled him over, he would of got up in the morning and everything would have been the same as always. That made her a murderer.

I half wanted the knife and half didn't. It used to belong to a chief who was a real good carver and what I wanted to be then was one of them carving Indians who get famous and drive a new car. That was the part that made me keep the knife. I sure wasn't excited about the magic part. I knew Angie had power over it just like she did over the guy who gave it to her. So I never told.

She couldn't tell no one either, not even the priest, maybe

especially not the priest. After our dad died, she started sleeping on the floor and not eating. Angie got so skinny she could hardly even hold a gun, which is why, when she went out under the tree and shot herself in the head, she missed everything but the smelling part of her brain.

They took the bullet out and she was home from the hospital in the time it took to wash and dry the clothes that had her blood all over them. That's what I remember, Angelina saying she was going to the woods to be with Mum and Dad and nobody stopping her because she was always saying stuff like that and then LaVerne washing her clothes afterward and the water in the washtub was all red like her blood.

Later on, they made jokes and said Angie put a gun in her mouth and blew out the taste and smell part of her brain because my sisters were such bad cooks.

3.
Making the River

I was making a river in the dirt, wasting the big tub of rainwater my sister LaVerne was saving to wash her hairs, and the water was as muddy as the Chemainus when the dog salmons come home for the winter. It was hot and LaVerne was pissed because her hairs were dirty, but it was too late. I already poured out most of the water and the rest was filled up with tadpoles I was saving to put in the river.

Laverne said she was so mad at me her hairs hurt and she sat down on the ground and lit up a big doobie and I said she better watch out 'cause I just seen the cops over at Ambrose's looking for that stolen bike and she said no problem she could swallow the joint like my cousin Alfred who swallowed a balloon that had dope in it.

My cousin Alfred told me balloons was simple to swallow as oysters. He got it back later, he said, easy as pie, but I didn't believe him because he was never right in the head and never told the truth so far as I remember. He ate too many balloons and got too much honky food in jail. Honky food is no good for Indians.

Indians need fish all the time. That's what keeps our bones warm in the winter.

Say you're goin' fishin' all the time
I'm a-goin' fishin' too.
Bet your life, your lovin' wife
Catch more fish than you.
Any fish bite if you got good bait.
Here's a little somethin' I'd like to relate -
Any fish bite if you got good bait.
I'm a-goin' fishin', Yes, I'm goin' fishin'
You can come a-fishin' too.

My cousin Alfred's girlfriend called Seattle Ruby told me this story about a five finger discount lady she heard about. This auntie had a diamond in her tooth and one day she swallowed it down with a big feed of corn. No problem, she got it back. I guess, you gotta be a real greedy person to look through your shit for a piece of fancy glass.

Alfred met Seattle Ruby when he went fruit picking with the Mexicans. She had a guitar and she taught us the words to all these songs, especially the fishing song, my favourite one, and she made real good chili. But she took off one time when he was in the slammer and she never came back on account of it was her that put him there after he beat her up. I was sorry about that because she was real nice to me when she wasn't drinking.

So I had this river starting up and LaVerne was sitting there bitching and scaring my pretend river fish, those bullfrog tadpoles I got over at the pond and I was thinking I wished she'd swallow a balloon and it would fill up with air and take her away someplace so I could play in peace and quiet.

I had all these plastic cowboys and Indians Ruby gave me for going to the store and getting her cigarettes. I mean, she didn't actually give them to me. She gave me a buck for myself and I got the soldiers and a bag of wax lips which nobody was gonna pike off me because they tasted like road tar.

My cowboys had guns and the Indians had bows and arrows which wasn't fair when you think of it but it didn't matter none to me because they were all guarding the river. They had to because this was the second batch of tadpoles. The first bunch got eaten up by Mabel Thomas' ducks which she had for the eggs.

Chicken eggs wasn't good enough for Mabel Thomas. I think she sent them over to eat my tadpoles because she was a high and mighty lady who thought she was better than other Indians on account of her husband had a job in the bush and a new camper and he was elected chief.

Mabel was real fat but her kids were skinny. Every morning she'd start stuffing her pie hole as soon as them kids were out the door. By the time they got home starving hungry from school, she'd be sleeping on her porch with one of them cowboy hand-kerchiefs they give out at big dances over her face and there'd be nothing left to eat.

Them ducks hid their eggs all over the place and Mabel sent the kids looking because she was too lazy to go after them herself. There was no way of knowing how old those eggs were. I'd be scared to eat one. You could hear her passing wind all the way to the road. It was the first thing we noticed when we got let off the school bus. We'd jump down and say to the Thomas kids "Your old lady's been eating rotten eggs again."

After the first tadpole massacre, I captured one of Mabel Thomas' ducks and put it in the toilet with the lid down. Boy did it holler. Here I am sitting on that toilet like it was a bucking bronco and LaVerne comes busting in and grabs me so hard the lid comes off with me and we both land on the floor on top of each other and the duck jumps out and shakes itself and walks out the front door and across the road to Thomas's as calm as if it had been to holy communion.

I don't think they were smart enough to think of it themselves on account of their brains were starving too and I never once saw those Thomas kids obey their mother, so I still haven't figured out who it was who hung my next bunch of bullfrog babies on the clothesline with clothes pegs in their tails and their heads lolling down and their eyes popping out.

If it was LaVerne, I guess I already fixed her and her big Saturday night date at the wrestling match. Her precious rainwater was about as useful to her as a bucket of tadpoles.

4.

My Secret

I didn't tell my secret to nobody. Ever since our mother went to spirit, I slept in the same bed with Lester. I got Lester's hand me down clothes and the old stuff Sister got from people at church. I went swimming with Lester, but he never seen me naked.

The river was my life. It was like a person to me. Sometimes the water was fast and full of mud and you couldn't tell what it was thinking except you knew it was hungry because those were the times the little children fell in, and you couldn't call them back because they were already gone with the fish people. I wondered if them kids were happy when they met up with their grandmothers and grandfathers in the ocean where the fish people hang out when they're not getting born or dying or leaving their eggs in the river.

I always liked to swim underwater the best. I could hold my breath for a long time and when I came up I heard the other kids saying "Where's Charlie?" It made me feel good that I fooled them like that and made them miss me so much they started up calling my name.

The only person that ever saw me naked was my mother and my sister LaVerne who looked after me the most and then Sister who helped me with vaseline when I caught myself in my zipper that time at school. But my peeper was all she saw. We never swam skinny in the river like the hippy kids on the farm across the railway tracks. We never had bathing suits like the Dutch Reform kids up by the bridge. All us Indians swam with our clothes on and we still swam faster than any of them white kids.

We were happy about that because it sucked going to school with them. The white kids got new clothes and new lunch kits every year and they had gym strip and they finished their work real quick and got gold and silver stars on their papers. When it came to running and swimming and art, we got to beat them good and that was fair enough.

I liked the river the best in the summer when all my brothers and sisters came down to wash their hairs. We did it in the time when the sun was red in the sky and the rocks were hot to lie on. I can still hear us laughing and splashing, filling the river with soap bubbles. We all had long hairs then and my sisters sold theirs sometimes to Simon Charlie for the masks he was carving, but it always grew back.

When we finished washing our hairs, we came out of the river and lay down on the rocks and spread them out to dry. I wondered what my late mother and father thought when they looked down on us lying there with our shining halos around our heads, just like pictures of Jesus. I hope they were happy then.

The other best time at the river was when the dogs came home. Then none of our kids went to school. Every day we went to the river with our jigs and our poles and the little guys copied the men only we couldn't lug them big fish home when we caught them.

The ranger got real mad and told us he was going to put us in jail for catching fish we didn't eat. That was on top of busting people for pit-lamping and catching deers at night. Soon they was gonna have all the Indians in jail and no one left to bust, so then that Ranger would be out of a job. And anyway what's the point of putting somebody in jail for doing something your father and your grandfather and your great grandfather did and taught you to do so your family could eat dinner and have skins for their drums?

Instead of chasing us with a gun, the Ranger could of helped us kids take our fish home in his jeep, but he didn't, and the men had enough fish of their own to take back to the smoker in the wheelbarrow that Alex, who was the dad in the white family I wanted to be in, loaned out to us.

That was then. The government guys got pissed off with Indian fishing and decided they would stop us all from going to the river for our food. They started turning up at Number 13 with a big truck full of fish and dumping it on a plastic sheet they put down on the road. You were supposed to go pick up your fish from this giant pile. What's the fun in that? You had to bend over for it and you felt like you had to say thanks for the fish and they were our fish in the first place. We liked going fishing. It was our way of life. Some people never stopped but some said what the heck if the honkies want to give us fish we'll take them and that was the end of a lot of kids learning about going to the river, which is the only thing my Indian father ever taught to me.

He gave me the river which is a lot more than I ever got from my real father who has all the money in the world.

My Indian father called me Son, never Charlie. I remember that. I don't think he ever saw me naked. I wanted to be a good son and a good fisherman. I wanted him to look down and be proud of me the way he was of Lester and Wally. I wanted the other kids to like me even though my parents were gone to spirit in a bad way and never got to be Elders. I never wanted to be different from the other kids. I wanted them to say my name like I belonged. I wanted to catch fish and carve wood and mind my own business and maybe meet my other family one day.

When my real father got married, the white family on the other side of the railroad tracks had this big potlatch. They killed two lambs and a lot of salmon and cooked them outside Indian style on an alder fire. My brothers Lester and Wally helped cut the wood.

My sister Rose fixed me a clean shirt and Alex came by with the tractor and the hay wagon and we all caught a ride over to the farm with him. It was a beautiful day when my real father got married. It made me mad that he didn't send me a message, but there was a big chance he didn't even know about me. I was happy to be going to his wedding, even though he didn't know about that either.

The lambs were already cooking when we got there. They had bales of hay in a circle around the fire and all the white people in town and some Indians were sitting around in fancy clothes drinking this special punch and looking at the fire.

Then this drunk guy played a tune on the trumpet and there was a bride and groom coming out of the house, but it was my farm brothers Gabe and Mitchell. Mitch was the groom and Gabe was dressed like a bride with this white ladies' dress and a long veil and flowers in his hair and he looked nice. It made me feel funny. They handed out flags and presents to all the kids. I got these special crayons and paper to draw on. The drunk guy who played the trumpet married them in the garden, then they kissed each other and everyone laughed because they liked it and it was the first time I ever felt OK about my secret.

After the wedding, there was a real feast. They had the lambs and some fish and potato salad and watermelon and the other kind of salad that honkies eat because their ancestors were all white rabbits with pink eyes.

When the men and women starting drinking plain liquor after dinner they forgot about the punch bowl that was ice carved up like a swan. It was real nice but the swan was melting and the punch tasted like all different kinds of fruit and it had flowers floating in it. I never saw anything like it in my life before. Us kids thought it was a real waste to let the swan melt away and all the punch would end up in the grass and the worms would get drunk and what was the point of that. It might as well be us.

The bride got drunk first and he threw up in a bush that had pink flowers in it. I can still see that bush. After he finished, it looked like it had that paper stuff they throw at weddings all over it. I thought that was the funniest thing I ever seen. Those people were so fussy about their flowers and their grass and then their kid went and threw up all over it. If they were Indians there wouldn't of been a fancy bush in the first place and the rain would have washed the throwup away. No problem.

I got drunk too. It was the first time. The farm started spinning around me and the sheep and the trees and the flowers and the people were all running together, so I lay down in the hay wagon and looked up at the stars and I saw the face of my real father and the lady he married that day and they were smiling at me and I smiled at them and then I was sick.

5.
M'Zelle

The St. Pierre's got a French side and an Indian side just like us Louies. Some of them got real pale faces and light coloured curly hair and some of them look like us. M'zelle's mum and dad both look like real hundred percent Indians with long black hairs but M'zelle herself looked more like Rose's baby after she bleached it. She had this fuzzy halo like baby Jesus and when she was a baby her dad threw her up in the air and he said "Are you an Indian?" and M'zelle laughed and laughed.

I don't know what her real name was. I don't think anybody remembers. One person started calling her that name and it gave M'zelle her heart's desire to go to France, which she did, but not the way she thought.

I was there when M'zelle got herself born. I heard her mum hollering in the back bedroom and I heard M'zelle's first crying. We were watching cartoons on the couch waiting for the baby to get born so her dad would give the big kids money to go get us all candy to celebrate.

He did and then he got drunk and M'zelle's half-sister had a baby nine months later, but that one was pure Indian.

M'zelle was two years younger than me but we stuck together like two dogs fucking, not that we ever did that. As soon as she could walk, M'zelle was following me around, even to the river. I made sure she got across the road without being hit by a car like some other kids we knew and I showed her how to pee outside without getting none of it on her shoes.

She was one of those real skinny girls that surprise everyone by turning out to be pretty after all. M'zelle must of been six feet tall. She was as tall as Joe Thomas and he was a high jumper. Her eyes were mud green and her hairs was the colour of dry grass. Even though they were curly, they were soft. I remember that.

For an Indian, M'zelle was good at school. I think she was the only one of us that got stars on her work. In the end, it was bad for her because they always said M'zelle will do this and M'zelle will do that, like going to university and getting to be a teacher or a lawyer or something. They always said M'zelle sure knows how to keep up her end of an argument, she will make a great speaker for our people. M'zelle will get our land back.

The truth is the only piece of land M'zelle ever got hold of for us Indians was a piece of sidewalk at the corner of Blanshard and View.

By the time M'zelle was twelve, they said she was jail bait and the big job they dreamed about was going down the toilet. Every guy in town was cruising the reserve hoping to get a look at her. You never heard anything like them horns honking and them tires squealing. M'zelle was going wild on us and nobody could think of a reason to keep her at school, not even the nuns. Soon as those guys in their cars cruised by the res, she'd be out her door and in the front seat before they could change gears.

The Elders was talking about grabbing her for the bighouse because she had the worst case of boy crazy they ever seen. M'zelle could of learned her grandmother's dance. She could of been a Raven, which was her grandmother's family.

But she never got to be anything but a girl that got to go to France. One day she got in a big black car and never came back. I guess she was about fifteen or sixteen by then.

The next time I seen M'zelle, she didn't even know me. We both looked a lot different. I guess she was using. She went back from being beautiful to being skinny all over again. The bones in her face was sharp as a knife. You could gut a fish with them bones. It was at the first day of spring. I remember the cherry trees blooming on the sidewalk. They were coming down like pink snow. I seen her standing there in front of that St. Andrew's Cathedral with her face pointed at the sun and her hands jerking in the air and the pink snow all around her. M'zelle looked right at me but she didn't see me.

I stood there for a long time under that cherry tree and I remembered the day M'zelle got born and the big bag of candies we kids got and the day she caught a big fish down by the bridge and she fell in the river but we got her and the fish out and the time she was Mary in the Christmas play and one of the parents was pissed off an Indian got to do it and said M'zelle had dirty fingernails and shouldn't touch the Jesus child, even if it was only a doll, and the day we painted our fingernails black and the day her hair got burned up and the day she left in that big black car with the top down.

She was standing there looking real mean in her black clothes and her black high heels and she gave me a dirty look because I was on her corner.

They said she made a total eclipse.

When I was in jail the guys used to look at the sun through

a tin can with holes in it. That made us high. So was M'zelle, who been to France with the man in the big black car or the man after him and they said she was a model there for a Paris designer, the same M'zelle who looked at the sun with me when we were little kids because someone told us not to, probably one of the nuns because they was always telling us not to do everything, especially if it was something we wanted to, like touch ourselves or walk into the bakery and take a whole pie and eat it right there on the road, which we did.

She went up the stairs to the very top of the parking lot, it must of been five or six different stairs altogether, so she had a lot of time to think about where she was going, and she stood there in her black clothes with her arms out like a big black bird and then she jumped and the sun was covered up for as long as it took for her eye to blink for the last time and then she landed on the sidewalk.

I heard this all from Tonto and he said the funny thing was he looked up and seen her there and thought how beautiful she was, and how she went to Paris and wore them clothes and here she was back doing her grandmother's dance on the roof of the Parkade and he knew he shouldn't be looking, but he did. He looked at her and he looked at the sun.

And when he looked down again, there was M'zelle lying on her piece of sidewalk and her little pink brain was somewhere's else a ways off and there's this black crow eating it and maybe that was the right thing after all.

6.
Me and M'Zelle Eat Cake

There was a couple of times me and M'zelle threw up together-er and those are special days because how many people can you say that about, eh? You can say you got drunk with somebody or you stole a car with somebody or you even stood on one side of the road and tried to pee over to the other side and see which guy could pee the farthest, but how many guys did you ever throw up with?

It was in the summer. Them kids at the farm had this pony and they said we could ride it whenever we wanted. M'zelle loved horses. When she got on that pony you couldn't tell which part was her and which part was horse.

That reminds me of a story Tom Louie told us kids. He comes from up north and it was about a carving he made before he moved down here to be with my Auntie Charlene. This carving was two bears fucking, the guy bear on top of the woman bear. The priest was admiring Tom's work and Tom decided he would take these two bears fucking to him because he helped Tom out of a five finger discount problem he was having with the

33

cops. The priest said it was a good carving but Tom better cut the guy off because it wouldn't look too good, the priest having a carving like that. He could get into trouble when the Bishop came for a visit.

So Tom he goes and cuts the guy off but he leaves his back legs and what the priest gets is a woman bear with six legs. He said the priest said it was nice and he never noticed. We laughed 'til the pee ran down our legs.

So me and M'zelle came running over after school and we rode that pony until it got dark and we couldn't see no more. April made us sandwiches and she said it made her feel good to see kids who liked her bread so much. Her own kids wanted bread from the store but I liked her bread better. The truth is I was glad to have any kind of bread, especially at the end of the month when all our money was gone and it wasn't Welfare Wednesday yet.

In the summer, the farm kids went to see their grandmother and me and M'zelle got money to look after the pony. We each got a buck a day and we had to make sure it had water.

That pony had the softest nose.

Just going over there made me hungry and I got to thinking about those sandwiches and the cookies April made too. There wasn't nothing much to eat at home. We had our last bag of baloney sandwiches at the river the day before. The little kids were crying like crazy. There's nothing noisier and more miserable than a kid with a noisy belly.

First of all, we took some carrots from the vegetable patch to the pony and we had some ourselves and I said we should take some home. It was M'zelle's idea to look in the barn. There was this freezer where they kept the lambs after they got killed. I said OK, why not, they always gave us something to eat when we went to visit. In fact, April called my cousin Star "Got any Cookies"

34

'cause that was the first thing she ever said when we went visiting there. As far as I know, they still call her by that name.

Me and M'zelle started in on this big bag of raisins. It was bigger than M'zelle herself. Them raisins were cold, but we didn't care. We ate handfuls and handfuls and then M'zelle spotted this cake in a box and it had roses on it and it said Happy Birthday. It wasn't neither of us' birthday but it looked so good with the fancy roses and it tasted good too. That cake had layers and layers with jam in between and it was so good we couldn't stop eating it until it was all gone.

And then M'zelle said "Remember the time all the kids from the res started going to the farm to tell April it was their birthday because they heard she gave me a present on mine?" All of a sudden, it was everybody's birthday. There must of been ten or more kids down there knocking on the door and saying guess what and she gave them each something to colour with or a book or maybe both. Then my cousin Joe who is just a little kid decides to go twice and ask for a birthday present.

So April gets us all over there on the back porch which I know is where she spanks her boys because I hear them hollering and she says to us kids "I may be white and I may grow grass that is not for eating or smoking, but I am not stupid." Then she tells us we better get our parents to make a list of whose birthday is when or she's going to quit giving us presents altogether and I tell her my parents are in heaven as if she didn't already know and she rolls her eyes and gives me one of those hard hugs that smell like bread cooking and my stomach growls. I wished then that me and April could run away to some place where I could be her real kid.

So me and M'zelle are laughing and stuffing our pie holes with frozen cake and I guess those raisins are puffing up inside us and I feel so full I just want to lie down in the hay for a minute but before I can do that I am doing the technicolour smile all over her shoes and the front of her dress.

The rest of them raisins came out the other end. When she figured out who done it, April said we sure made a mess of her outhouse and somebody better clean it up. She said there was twenty-five pounds of raisins in that there bag and she made the cake for her mother who was coming over to visit when they got back from the other grandmother's. I sure felt bad about that but M'zelle started to laugh and then I started too and pret'soon all three of us was laughing our heads off.

April said we were truth challenged candy criminals and it was bad luck to steal a birthday cake, so we better think about that, but I seen she couldn't stop laughing so I knew we were in the clear.

I wish I could tell you that was the end of it, but it wasn't. One night at the end of the summer, we got our bad luck. There was this big storm. Some of the roof came off our house and all the kids were holding on to each other under the blankets. In the morning, me and M'zelle went over to see the pony and it was lying down. There was this lamb standing beside it, licking it, but it didn't get up. April said it had a heart attack because it was scared of the wind, but I know why it happened. April already told me it's karma if you do a bad thing, then another bad thing comes after it.

7.
What Happened
On Mother's Day

I never get to drive that much in a car. A lot of people just drive by when Indians try to catch a ride someplace. You got to eat dirt when they drive up on the shoulder. Sometimes they throw bottles out the window and you got to duck them.

I like to feel the wind in my face. My sister Rose says I'm like one of them dogs that rides in the back of trucks. When I was a kid, I helped out on Alex's tractor and caught a ride whenever I could, but I never did like the school bus.

Me and M'zelle sat in the back of Auntie Charlene's car one day she was taking some of his carving down to the museum and we thought up this game about kissing. You had to think up this thing and then dare the other person to do it. Mayzelle dared me to kiss this snake she had in her pocket, and I did.

One time I told her about this bird I seen that flew into the window because it saw the sun shining in the glass. It broke its neck and died and there was this mark on the window where the bird smacked it. The mark had feathers stuck to it. M'zelle said the bird kissed the window. She dared me to do it and I did and then she did. She said we both kissed something dead and that was our secret. The day M'zelle left for Paris, she kissed the inside of the window in the big black car and she had lipstick on. When I think about her, I see her lips on the glass.

I never kissed M'zelle. I never wanted to do that, even though she asked me to put a pencil inside her one day in the bushes. She said she learned that from one of the honky girls at school, who had a fort for playing doctor, but I never seen her play with the white girls, so she must have made that up or learned it from one of her uncles.

One other time we played make a wish and when we went over the bridge we lifted up our legs and held our breath. M'zelle told me her wish and it came true. She said she wanted to get away from here.

That time we were in the taxi, my brother Wally asked the bootlegger to bring him a bottle and we caught a ride back to his place. It was too bad they put him in jail for driving the taxi and bringing the bottles to our people because that was when Sam and them drank the Gestetner fluid from the residential school over there on Kuper Island and died.

Sam was Mary Joe's kid, the only one she had left after one died in a car crash and the other got burned up that time her cabin caught on fire. Mary had Sam and Them, who were all the guys who hung out with him at her house. She let Them watch her TV and she made them supper. Sometimes she got mad at Them when they stole the money she made from making her baskets.

When Mary got sick with cancer, she was asking for this medicine from one of them yew trees, but they couldn't find the guy who made it. He had another wife in Seattle and nobody

38

knew where she lived, especially the wife who lived here. She would of had one of her cousins deliver some poisoned moose meat if she could of found out where she was at. They took Mary to the hospital and Sam and them went on a real bender. They didn't like Mary bossing them around but she was like a mother to all of them, even if she did get mad sometimes and chase them with a stick.

She mostly chased her husband who liked to look at other women on account of he was younger than Mary, a lot younger. Mary dyed her hair and did all this other stuff to make him happy like cooking beaver, but he still looked at those kloochmas.

On Mother's Day, they got real upset thinking she was going to die and nobody had any booze. The taxi guy was in jail for bootlegging. Sam went out on the road and collected some bottles but he didn't have enough and besides there was no one to drive the taxi to take them to town.

Then someone gets this bright idea to take this leaky old boat out to the island and see what was around the school. The school was a bad place. All them nuns were gone because they beat the kids and did other mean things to them and the priest too. I know all about that. Some kids ran away. One tried to row on a log and he drownded and his sister too.

The good thing about the school was that it was unlocked and you could just help yourself to anything you liked. No one wanted the old books, especially the Bibles. Some of the guys made a real mess of the chapel. They broke all the windows and relieved themselves on the holy books. The people on the island burned the furniture in the winter time. Some of it turned up at Val Vil.

The first time I come to Donna's place there's this chair I remember seeing at the school. Donna says sit down and I say no. I was gonna stand up or sit in some other chair but not that one.

That one had evil spirits all over it. Maybe some Indian kid got laid across it and had his ass beat for speaking to his own sister at recess time. Maybe worse.

Sam had this idea if they could get to the island they could drink this stuff that was in the office. It had liquor in it. Then they wouldn't feel so bad about Mary's cancer which was making her bring up all this black stuff and talk in her old language which nobody here understands. They was scared.

I never remembered my mother except for seeing her float out of the car that night and Mary was real nice to me, more like a mum than a auntie, so I went by her place on Mother's Day with some flowers I picked for Sam and them to take to the hospital in case they could catch a ride there. The cabin was real quiet. I figured Sam and them already went to see Mary, but what they was really doing was crossing over in this leaky boat and borrowing the gestetner fluid from the nuns who weren't there no more.

It's too bad they weren't because they might of chased the boys with long rulers and stopped them from drinking that stuff. The next morning I heard all of them died from the poisoning, all except Larry's girlfriend, Cathy Thomas, who didn't like the taste of it because it reminded her of school.

8.
Sassy

This is what happened. Mary Joe's husband, who she hit with a stick every time he looked at another kloochma and had to go around with his head down and his hairs all over his face so he looked like a Sasquatch and everyone called him Sassy after that, he got in a taxi and went all the way to Nanaimo to the Woodward's Mall to buy her coffin clothes. She didn't have a nice dress and he promised and so that was it. He blew a month's cheque on a taxi and a dress and the booze he needed for the bender after her funeral. Sassy never drove so far in a car in his life. I heard the driver, who was our bootlegger fresh out of jail, made him pay up front just in case he disappeared like the time the boys all got their bottle money together and sent him into the booze store to get a tank of red.

Sassy got this smart idea when he ran into April that time and decided to catch a ride on her skirt and beat it with the bottle before the guys in the jungle caught on. April sure didn't know one end from the other and by the time she had the key in the ignition there was these mad Indians climbing on the back of her truck. She was driving along with those guys yelling and banging on the window and Sassy in the passenger seat drinking as fast as he could right out of the bottle. I guess she figured Alex would take care of it when she got home with her load of mad Indians.

I seen them drive past the res; April looking pissed off, Sassy smiling in the front seat and Sam and Them sliding back and forth when she hit the curves. Before long, the whole town knew about it. Everyone but Sam and Them was laughing their heads off.

They even had another big fight at Mary's funeral.

Sassy didn't buy a dress after all. He got talked into this pantsuit thing that was on sale at Woodward's. It was sort of a blue colour with silver threads in it. There was a scarf around her hair. It was a different blue. She looked real peaceful, almost as if she knew Sassy went to all this trouble to make her look nice after that suffering with the cancer in her stomach.

April got all the baskets she could and filled them up with wildflowers. She got daisies and lupin and forget me nots and wild sweet peas and I don't know what else, all these flowers Mary liked. It was extra sad because Mary didn't have any boys left to cry for her, so everyone else cried harder. You never saw so much carrying on in that church, but it looked beautiful with the sun coming through them stained glass windows and the colours all landing on Mary's baskets with the summer flowers in them.

By the time the priest got started they collected enough money for two funerals. Then there's this loud noise on the gravel and it's the guys from up north where Mary come from. They were late and they had it in their heads to take Mary back to their place where she was born and bury her there.

The brawling started outside and it sounded like big dogs humping little dogs with the wailing inside and the arguing outside between the guys from up north and the money collectors who wanted to bury her next to Sam and Them, who died for her.

The guys from up north came in the church and grabbed her coffin and we never saw Mary again. That made Sister and April the only ladies I got left.

Now Sassy lives on that corner downtown. He's the guy with the buttons all over his hat and his coat and he played the harmonica until somebody stole it. They took his chair too. He had a chair to sit on and enjoy the sunshine but the guys who own the stores down there didn't want a panhandling Indian feeling too comfortable so they took it away. Now he sits on the sidewalk with his sore leg straight out in front of him.

Sassy saw M'zelle jump too and he just said she looked pretty up there in the sky and it reminded him of those eagles down by the river that got shot by the honkies. One minute they were eagles with their big wings up covering the sun so you could see every feather and the next they were dead.

Sister Mary Joseph said everyone who is sorry gets to be an angel. I figure we all turn into clouds. Sometimes I lie on the ground and look up and I can see all those people. I see my mother and Mary and M'zelle and my father and the princess who was married to my real father and went to spirit because he didn't love her. I see them all. Fog is clouds on the ground. What I like to do is walk into fog. I like to touch it and feel it touch me. It hurts but not as bad as some things I could mention, like being hit in the jaw so hard your teeth fall out.

9.
The Floating Bridge

Me and M'zelle were hanging out on the floating bridge at Loon Lake feeding seeds we got five finger discount from Alex's feed bin to the ducks and watching the bugs. The bug I liked best looked like them planes that land on water that Sister Mary Joseph called a Damsel Fly and Sister Marie Therese called a Ladies' Needle. Them two was always arguing and sometimes it was about me.

Sister Marie Therese made me stand in the corner when I couldn't read off the blackboard. I had to stand there after school too. My body was shaking because I didn't have nothing to eat that day. She kept me in at lunch and I didn't get over there to the convent for my sandwich. Sister Marie Therese said I was stubborn and kids like me gave Indians a bad name and it hurt her because she was part Indian too and if she could learn to read, I could learn to read.

She sat there with a big apple on her desk and she wouldn't budge and I was so hungry my mouth was dry. I was hurting for that apple and I can still see it now. It was red and shiny on one

44

side and green on the other. She said she was going to keep me in until Hell froze over and then I saw this nice picture in my mind. Old Sister Marie Therese was bare naked in the snow with icicles hanging from her nose. My sister LaVerne told me that you should always imagine a person naked when they were mean to you. Believe me, Sister Marie Therese was not a pretty sight. You couldn't even make soup out of her skinny bones.

Anyways, about dark time, in comes Sister Mary Joseph and she is hopping mad, all four and something feet of her. She picks up Sister Marie Therese's whacking ruler and starts chasing her around the desk. I got the hell out of there and I skipped school for the rest of the year after that. It was only about the first haying time so that added up to a lot of school.

I pass a lot of time looking at things. I guess the days me and the other kids sat by the river watching the fish and the times I went to the lake were the best in my life.

This one time, M'zelle was watching these water bugs fucking and she gets the idea she would like to try it with me, right there in broad daylight. Considering she was just a kid and I sure wasn't into it, the whole idea was crazy. I told her if I fucked her I'd have to marry her and look what happened to all the cousins who got married. Their kids were crazier than they were and did things like fucking each other at the floating bridge when they should of been looking at bugs.

M'zelle said she wanted to know if it was different doing it with a friend and I knew what she meant by that. She said she never kissed nobody and I knew about that too because I had that done to me and not a kind word or a kiss or nothing.

M'zelle had this big leaf and she was kissing it because she said the fuzz on the leaf was like a boy's face. She was licking it and everything. She said when the time came that somebody kissed her she was going to be good at it.

The lake was still and that green that comes after winter that makes your insides hurt. It felt like you just seen a kitten with its eyes shut. The water was soft and thick as the green jelly Sister made on St. Patrick's Day. The ducks cut through it though. They were diving for minnows. With the five finger discount seeds and the baby fish, they got a good lunch that day.

Dragonflies do it in the air. I seen airplanes do tricks on TV but that is nowhere near as beautiful as dragonfly love. The guy one kind of hooks the girl one while she's flying and holds her there. When he lets go, she flies down to the water and drops her egg.

I felt sorry for M'zelle when she told me one of our uncles did it to her and never kissed her. I wasn't going to kiss her to make it better, but I showed her something I bet she never forgot even if she didn't know who I was on the street in front of the cathedral that day. I showed her how to catch a dragonfly. I made my hand move like a leaf on a tree as it came up to this lazy guy sleeping in the sun. He never knew what hit him. A chameleon I saw on TV learned me that and I showed her.

10.
My First Communion

I never told anyone before what happened with Father Jim. It started with him noticing my two eyes were different and he made a joke about it. He was calling me the little devil. He told me that old story I already heard from Sister about two different eyes meaning you were possessed by the devil and the church people used to burn you at the stake for that. I was never possessed by nothing except what I seen at the Bighouse when the dancers get the spirit and that would be the bear or the eagle or whatever was in your family comes in your body so you can dance. My family is Raven like M'zelle's.

I been a bird from time to time, especially in my dreams. In my dreams, when something bad is happening, I can open my wings and fly any place I want to. Sometimes I fly over the Bighouse my real father lives in. I can see right down the chimneys into it. It is a pret'house with soft beds and lots of blankets and fires in lots of rooms. I can see my brothers riding horses in the garden.

Father was in school for our catechism classes and he told

me I better come by the rectory for extra lessons on account of I couldn't remember everything the way I was supposed to and maybe that was because there was a bit of devil in me.

He gave me lunch too. It was better than Sister's lunch, because she had to teach all day and he had a special Sister for making it and she gave him a pudding on top of the sandwich. On cold days, there was soup or maybe macaroni, which I liked because there was lots of cheese on it.

I told Father my blue eye came from my real father and not the one he buried. Father looked surprised and his one eyebrow went up but he didn't ask me who my real father was, so I didn't tell him. I didn't figure it was nobody's business but mine and maybe Sister's on account of she had the pictures. I had one or two things all my own, or mine and my true friends, and that was my secrets and my book April gave me for keeping pictures.

Father said adultery was a sin and I wasn't sure what that was but I acted like I did so he would let me go back to regular school because it was the afternoon by then and we were doing gym in the afternoon and gym and art were two things I liked at school.

Other boys had special lessons with Father, but we never went at the same time. I thought it would be a good idea if we went together but then I had the idea Father might not give us all lunch if there was a bunch of us, so I kept my mouth shut about that.

He told me about other sins too and they had to do with touching myself which would make me blind like Seattle Ruby's baby brother, but I done it anyway and I never went blind. Not yet.

Father was real nice to me. He gave me chocolate bars and he took me to the circus and one day he took me to this movie. He got one bag of popcorn and two cokes. I don't even remember what movie it was because right at the start of it he told me to

48

have some popcorn and when I put my hand in the bag there was something alive in it. Holy! Father said to just touch it and I didn't want any popcorn after that. I just sat there in the dark with my hand stuck in the bag because I didn't know what to do about it.

On the way home, I didn't look at Father and he said now we had two little secrets between us, the first one being about my real father. The next time I had special class, I skipped and went to the river, but Father came to the res and told my brothers and sisters I would go to hell if I didn't take confirmation classes, so they made me go back because our mum and dad are buried in the Catholic cemetery and if I wanted to ever see them again I better get confirmed.

All the time I am thinking maybe I should go and find my real father and he could take care of all this business and we could ride horses together and I wouldn't have to ever see Father Jim again.

Father said what we did was not a sin, it was natural and what God meant us to do but it was a secret and I would go to hell if I ever told. I never did and I kept going there and Father kept giving me stuff, but part of me was mad at him because I didn't like what he made me do. When I got confirmed, I couldn't swallow the host. It stayed in my mouth and my mouth felt so full of it I thought I would choke right there in church so my sisters made a joke that I couldn't even eat the bread of angels and maybe our mother baked it up there because she liked to cook fry bread when she wasn't too drunk to start the fire going.

I couldn't spit my mother out, eh?

When I was finished with First Communion, he told me I still needed to come for special classes on account of my one eye

49

was still blue and my other eye was still brown and I said I would but I knew I wouldn't and I didn't. Father got hold of me by coming over to the res and he told me he got me some paints and brushes because God wanted me to paint and that's all. Nothing else was going to happen. I thought it was a promise. He crossed his heart and his eyes got red and filled up with tears, so I went to the rectory and got them but he told me to do those things again. It made me mad, but I didn't tell him. I just did it and then I said I had to pee and I took some pills from his bathroom.

I came back one night when he was at a wedding and I went in the bathroom window. I got all these church papers together on the carpet and I lit them on fire. Then I pissed on the fire. It was a little fire and it went out, but the carpet was all black and wet. That was the start of my great career. I went home and got into bed and touched myself and God never made me blind.

I forgot about church after that. Father never came after me again so I guess he knew who it was but he never called the cops or nothing, not then anyway. That was gonna be my third secret.

11.
The Fourth Secret

All my life I seen people hurting other people and some of them being kind. Sister Mary Joseph, she was kind, and my sisters and brothers too. It wasn't their fault when they had little kids that they gave them the food I should of got. I was lucky Sister liked me enough to give me sandwiches.

I was lucky my sisters and brothers never beat me up or pushed me down the steps like I seen happen in other people's families. I was just invisible to them sometimes, especially at the end of the month when the food money was all gone and the little kids were screaming for food. They didn't care what time I went to bed so long as I didn't bug them by changing the channels on the TV or making a racket. They didn't care if I went to school or not. Indians don't learn much at school. What's the point of learning that you're stupid and all the other kids are going to get everything in life starting with those gold stars on their work? I went to school for the sandwiches and when we got to do sports and art.

Only one time I did something mean. There was this kid,

Frankie, and he talked funny. He couldn't say some of the letters and the kids got him to say things and they laughed at him. He said stuff like fwench fwies and fwowed up.

Sister had him in for talking lessons after school and one time some of the kids waited until he came out of the school. They took this collection and I found a nickel on the road so I gave it in to the pool because I wanted to be with them. They gave Frankie the money and told him to go to the store and ask for dry curd cottage cheese, because he couldn't say C. Gee, I can hardly say it myself.

The next day, everyone at school knew that Frankie went to the store and asked for dry turds and they were telling him his eyes were brown 'cause he was full of shit and he went bawling to Sister Mary Joseph and Sister said she was going to paddle the guys that did it, only Frankie never told. Maybe he was scared he couldn't say our names right.

I felt bad and I five fingered a bag of jawbreakers and gave them to him at recess, but that wasn't even half as bad as what happened to M'zelle when the girls beat up on her.

There was this sock hop at the end of grade seven. M'zelle was the pret'girl in the school by then even if she didn't have a party dress as fancy as some of them others. All the guys wanted to dance with her, even the honkys. They didn't care if she was way taller than them. You could tell they wanted to lie their heads down right on her tits, but Father was there making sure nobody danced too close. Boys and girls was a whole diff'rent story to him.

You could see them other girls were mad. They stood in a row on the other side of the gym from the guys, waiting to be asked. The teachers said the boys could only get a do-nut if they danced. Some did. Some didn't. Not me. The girls would of said no or pretended they didn't hear me. That was one of the times I should of been invisible.

The guys that promised ate their do-nuts real slow and then asked the girls right near the end of the song. You could practically smell them girls burning. It was a bad smell like wet hairs and old tires on the fire at the garbage dump. Some of them danced with each other.

When all the food was gone and it was time to go home, a bunch of them go up to M'zelle and ask her real sweet to come back to their place for a sleep-over. M'zelle never heard of such a thing. She was in heaven. She smiled so hard her face was broke in half like that Bible sea the Sisters talked about. I didn't like the looks of it, but I high-tailed it out of there before Father started in asking me if I would like a glass of lemonade or some kind of special class over at his place.

That was another mistake I made because the next time I saw M'zelle she was as bald as a baby eagle and she told me them girls cut off her hair on the short cut through the woods and they burned it.

M'zelle never made it to high school and pret'soon the guy in the big car came and took her away.

My next fire was in a beauty parlour and it was for her.

12.
The Indian Hotel

One night April got mad at the kids for bad mouthing the dinner she was making and she got this big stack of plates out of her warming oven and dropped them on the floor. You should of seen their faces. They looked like somebody called off Christmas. Me too. I been hanging around waiting for her to tell me to wash my hands and sit down with the family and I sure didn't have no problem with turnips and potatoes and some meat from them lambs, but that meal was over before it started. As soon as the kids smelled sheep, they started saying baa to their mum.

I don't know why, but April was dressed funny for making dinner that time. She was standing over the wood stove with her hair falling down and this white nightie with lace on it. I thought it was a dress. I thought she was going out dancing with Alex, but he was smoking a joint on the porch pretending it wasn't stew and the kids were just a bad dream.

April gets her purse and she slams out the door and I take one look back at the kids and the three of them are sitting there at the table like they was a bunch of totem poles with their mouths hanging open. If I wasn't so hungry and mad about missing supper I would of laughed and that would of got them all started in laughing, but I didn't. I just followed April down the road, eating her dust. She sure did look funny riding her bike past them fields full of sheep with her nightie on and her rubber boots and her purse swinging over the handlebars.

When I got to the end of the driveway, she already hopped off her bike and unlocked the mailbox. I guess she had to check the mail to see if there was any money or useful lady samples in it before she ran away. I hid in the dog roses and got my legs scratched real bad, but I didn't want April to see me just yet when she was still that mad at boys. I was hoping she might ask me to go with her when she cooled out.

April had these cousins in England. She showed me pictures of where they lived and it was nice. You never know, they could of met my real dad. Her cousins could introduce me to him and the Princess and we could be one happy family riding around in one of them golden coaches you see on TV.

Speaking of coaches, along comes my uncle Ambrose on his bike and he was not waving. Not waving meant he was drunk. I seen him get off his bike and kind of fall on April and she was laughing and telling him to stand up or she was going to have to blow her whistle, but she didn't have to because I was coming out of the bushes to save her from Ambrose. Along came the fuzz at the same time with their lights flashing.

Too bad it was daylight saving and not dark yet, because April was lying beside the road in her messed up nightgown with her letters in her hand and I was on top of Ambrose who was on top of her and everyone could see.

The cops pulled me off first and then him and there she was and she wasn't wearing anything under her nightie which was up around her bum by this time.

That was my first night at the Indian Hotel. First they took April home. Her kids was still sitting at the table and Alex had red eyes from the dope and he was sweeping up the broke china. He said the dishes was a wedding present with real gold around the edge and she was a mental case. The cops asked him polite to make sure she was dressed proper next time she went to check her mail and then me and Ambrose got taken into town and booked even though she said I didn't have nothing to do with it and Ambrose was probably only trying to be a gentleman, which fucked up because he was drunk and couldn't keep his balance. But the cop said he was sober enough to ride his bike and that was that. He got charged and April had to get one of her brothers who was a lawyer to get him off.

I got dinner that night, not do-nuts like the time I ran away to Campbell River, but sardines and toast. I don't know what happened to April's lamb stew.

All I had on was a T-shirt and jeans and it was cold in there. The cops gave me this thin blanket and I tried to get warm, but I couldn't. I could of cuddled up with Ambrose, but he stank and he snored and I just waited until morning. You could see out the window even though it was high up in the cell and I seen a bunch of stars and they were beautiful so maybe one of them was the light in my mother's place. It seems I spent my whole life being cold. I guess I'm used to it.

I like it when there is a light on and you can walk up to it and know someone is there waiting for you. Somebody like my mum or April or Sister. I thought if it rains tonight, then she seen me there. I used to think that rain was when angels cried and maybe it's true.

56

I thought about all the lights in the castle where my real father lives and how I nearly got there that time. If only Ambrose didn't come along and the cops too, then me and April would be on an airplane right now and we'd be on our way to London and I'd be waving out the window at my mother and my real father would be waving at me from that there red carpet they use for big shots.

The next time I went to jail, I remembered about them stars but I didn't get a cell with a window in it. Me and some of the guys made this way to get high when we went out to exercise. You make holes in cardboard and then you look right at the sun. You see these spots like stars and after a while you start to feel better.

13.
The First Time

What I stole from Father Jim that time was them holy
wafers he kept in the bathroom. Me and M'zelle and
Starlene Thomas went to the lake and we swallowed
them with some pop and Starlene left her mouth open too long
so a wasp flew in and stung her on the tongue. She was lucky her
tongue didn't swell up and kill her the way it did to her dad Bob
Thomas when he ate that jam sandwich on the log boom.

The holy wafers went down real nice and we laid down on
our backs and waited while the sky got white and fluffy and the
insects made music. The sun was smiling. The boards on the float
were warm and I said it was lucky there was a rail because I could
of gone to sleep and rolled into the green jelly and sunk right to
the bottom of the lake. Starlene didn't say nothing because of her
tongue hurting, but M'zelle says what's the difference the bottom
of the lake was beautiful and green and sleeping with fishes was-
n't a bad thing, not as bad as being an Indian.

We were warm and sleepy and I was the first one to yawn and
the holy wafers must of been magic because I had this feeling down

58

there. I never touched or anything, not with those two girls there. After a while, I said for them to yawn too, just open their mouths wide and Star didn't want to or she couldn't but M'zelle did and she was making these soft little moans and I knew she was feeling it too, but I didn't tell her my first secret, not with Starlene there.

M'zelle said I should go back to Father and get some more, but I never went back there after the fire. I was scared of what he might do, even though what he already done was as bad as I could think of.

I never did the white powder with her, but I could see she found it herself the way she was jiggling and twitching around in front of the bishop's house that day I saw her and she didn't know who I was except for just another hooker on her property.

That was different. I did it with Tonto who died a short time later on account of the China White being so strong, stronger even than Tonto who was from the North and real tough from working up there until he screwed his back up. That was the end of it for me when Tonto died. I didn't want to go to spirit that way, not with my mother looking down.

Tonto told me this stuff would make me feel good and it did and it didn't. I got sick. I was like laughing and throwing up at the same time. Tonto said you called it a technicolour smile. I was liquid laughing all over the sidewalk and all over my shoes, but the good thing was the whole world was a soft garden and it didn't matter that no one could see me.

The street was all flowers and trees and nothing ugly or hard. I was a flower opening up in my pink dress from Value Village, which M'zelle called Maison V.V. before she went to France and forgot everything she knew about the river, and it was all coming out of me so in the end I didn't feel mad at anyone, not even Father, and you could of given me a box of matches and I wouldn't know one end from the other.

When Alex and April split up and they sold the farm, me and them boys got together all the toys we could find and we put them in the sandbox they had when we were little kids and it was like a city. There was Lego and Playmobil and a wooden train set and all the stuff I saw them get for Christmas and I'm not saying I didn't get any, because I did. I mostly got stuff April thought I needed, like rubber boots and sweaters she knit with one arm shorter than the other and paint boxes and things like that. They hardly ever gave me toys, except for the second hand bike Alex fixed up for me and a soccer ball.

Me and the kids got all this junk together and we lit up a big doobie and laughed like crazy and played hard like little kids, then Gabe he went off to the gas station. They had this gas station for the farm and it had coloured gas in it you couldn't use in your car. He gets this big bucket full of gas and pours it all over the toys and then he lights a match and boom the whole thing goes up like in a movie. I could tell they liked it too. They lit that fire because they were hurting mad at somebody and we didn't need to talk about it. We just sat back and watched all them toys turn into ashes and puddles, just like Alex and April's marriage, I guess. I sure don't know what she was bitching about. Alex never beat her up. Heck, he hardly ever even talked to her.

That was the day we really got to be friends and it wasn't your stuff and my stuff or my pony and my parents, or them getting to be the Royal Family at the wedding party because they were honkys and went to the other church the Queen goes to. It was like we saw inside of each other and it was bad, but nobody cried. We laughed our heads off.

14.
Say My Name

When me and my brothers and sisters went to Oregon to pick fruit with our cousins down there, we met up with lots of Mexicans and Gypsies. The Mexicans are Indians too and we ate their food. It was good. We always had enough to eat when we went picking because there was the fallen down fruit that had bruises on it and then there was tortillas. Them Mexican ladies always had a big pot of beans going and you wrapped the beans in the tortilla and ate it together.

There was Gypsies too and the Mexicans and Gypsies played their guitars at night and they danced around the fire. We had full bellies and we laughed and told stories. That's how my cousin Alfred, the first guy I knew from jail, got together with Seattle Ruby who left him when he got mean. It was lucky they didn't get any kids to be broke in half.

I seen babies get born there all the time. Those women and their kids all picked fruit and when it was time for the baby to come they laid right down there in the orchard and had it. The other women helped, but the men kept on minding their own business and told jokes while that was going on.

I liked the girl stuff. I liked the dresses dancing around the fire and the smell of those women. When me and the farm kids dressed up and played kings and queens and had tea in Mitchell's bedroom, I wanted to be the queen. Gabe told me he read in a book that there was this guy that lived on a mountain and his name meant Ocean of Mercy. He said I could be him because he wore a dress all the time.

I didn't tell anyone when my tits started to hurt.

What one of the fruit Gypsies told me was a Gypsy has three names. There was the one your mother whispered in your ear when you got born and that was a secret and there was the one the Gypsies called you and then there was the one everyone else called you. I wondered if the Gypsy kids got confused, but I guess it was better than no one calling you anything because you just weren't a human being to them.

In jail, they call you by your last name. There are so many of my people there, it gets to be a joke. At roll call they say Louie, Louie and Louie because there was always somebody else called Louie who was one of my cousins in for something.

We had fun with the cops and the rangers on the res on account of nobody had their own home and you could be your cousin as far as they knew. They couldn't tell one Indian from another. If you done something bad or maybe shot yourself a deer which was not bad and the cops came riding up to your front door with all their lights on you just went out the back door and slept at somebody else's for a while. They got all these Indians lined up and asked them where so and so was and nobody knew nothing.

This was what happened to April that time we ate the birthday cake and the raisins. I was going to the river with a bunch of my cousins and April asked who ate all that stuff in the freezer without permission and who made a mess of the outhouse. We all said "I never" when April asked us until it got to little Angie and she turned to Thomas, who was next to her, and said "He did it," because she was too little to know any better, only he didn't. It was me and M'zelle, like I said before. Little Angie got whupped by her sister and she never did that again. She learned her about being an Indian. I wished April had spanked me with her wooden spoon that time because then I would of been one of her real kids and it might have saved that pony that died of fright in the lightning storm.

Once there was this lady ranger that was just starting out in her job. She thought she was smarter than the other ranger guys so she came along to the river with this bag of jelly do-nuts and she asked us who was who and who caught what fish and if we told her she gave us one of her do-nuts. We filled up our bellies and told her lies, but it took her a while to figure that out. Then she stopped bringing them.

Once I was at the river eating one of her do-nuts and this otter comes right up to me and takes it out of my hand. Nobody believes that but when I looked in its eyes they were green and I swear it was my mother. That was after Father Jim done what he done and I was getting tired of the angel stories.

I was waiting for this otter to lean into my ear and whisper my father's name, which was the one she gave me anyway, but she didn't. Maybe she thought twice wouldn't be lucky. Anyway, we're Indians, not Gypsies, and we got different stories.

Tonto from the North told me this story about Otter. He said Wolverine is his brother. He said his people hid their children at night because Wolverine stole them and raised them for food. Maybe all the wolverines was mothers that died and just wanted a baby for their own. I never told him that because I just thought of it and Tonto O.D.'d over a year ago.

He told me this other story about one time the Earth was made. That was when this guy had the boat with all the animals in it. Wolverine gets Otter to dive down after the big flood and get a mouthful of this world. Everyone knows Otter is a big pig so when he comes up, he won't give the mud up. So Wolverine blows in his bumhole and the Earth flies out of Otter's mouth.

Maybe that's how my mother got me. Maybe she left the Big Dance and went to the river where the Queen's son was down looking at Moon and she ate some dirt. Maybe, when her husband beat on the rear end of her with a stick for doing that, she just spat me out.

Indians get two names. You've got your honky name and that goes on your birth certificate and your pog money and that. Then there's your Indian name which comes from your grandfather or someone in your family. You might get that person's song and their dance when they grab you and take you to the Bighouse.

I only got one name and that was Charlie, but I know my mother whispered Charles in my ear the night I was born and the night she died in the car. If there is one thing I remember from being a baby, that was it. That night was cold and the windows were all froze up. You could see the ice on them and it was beautiful. My mother was drunk and she was dying, but she said Charles over and over and that's my name and I don't care about no other, not even the Indian name I never got.

Some people might say I was too small to remember my mother in the moonlight and the frost on the windows, but I do. Some things you just know in your heart. When the wind blows through the trees I hear my mother say my name. That makes me feel good. To most people, I'm just an Indian.

April, she told me this story one day about going into the

post office and hearing one of the cops talk about some guy buying it on the railroad tracks the night before. "Lucky it was just an Indian" the cop said about this squished guy and April says she went plate breaking crazy. She said "That's a human being you're talking about" and she up and belted him with her purse which I know for a fact was heavy, because she kept everything from all her silver money to a mopping up the kids rag and her spanking spoon in there.

In deer season, it looks like musical chairs down at the res, with the cops and Rangers going in one door and Indians running back and forth out the other. All's fair in love and war. That's what April told me. If they are going to put us in jail for being Indians, then we got a right to fight.

I never got a name dance on account of both my parents dying before they could make ends meet. To give a dance you got to buy gifts to give the guests and that adds up to a lot of money. You got to buy blankets and boxes of oranges and handkerchiefs and all this plastic stuff for the kitchen and then on top of that you give them money and feed them all too. It took my brothers and sisters ten years to save enough to give a picture dance for my parents after they died. They forgot about me, so I'm just Charlie and that's OK.

The first time I met Donna, she said "ends meat" is the part of the salami nobody wants to buy so they sell it cheaper. That was before we made our deal that didn't have nothing to do with money.

15.
What Rose Did

We should of known my crazy sister Rose would do it. She started shooting animals that weren't for eating and nailing them on the door of our house. There was all kinds of animals; squirrel, raccoon, that kind of thing. I told Rose squirrel is our friend and she sniffs at me and says "Squirrels are rats with cute tails and rats eat babies." By then, her arms were red and raw down to the bone from cleaning and there was no word about her baby at all.

It was as good as vanished with all the scrubbing.

We called those blackboard brushes the Sisters had Booboo Sticks, on account of they wiped out the mistakes you made. If only it was that easy for kids that don't belong. You could get wiped out by a big soft brush and turn into a puff of chalk and it wouldn't hurt at all, not like your mother washing you with bleach or some guy making you bend over a table while he sticks his egg beater up your ass and won't even say your name.

Grandpa died last week,
And now he's buried in the rocks,
And everyone still talks about
How badly they are shocked.
But me, I expected it to happen.
I knew he'd lost control
When he built a fire on Main Street
And shot it full of holes.
Oh, Mama can this really be the end,
To be stuck inside of Mobile
With the Memphis Blues again.

Seattle Ruby sang that song about holes in the fire. I know what she meant now. She meant safe places. There aren't so many of those. You got to find them yourself like Fire Woman who dances with flaming sticks and walks in the coals. She says she knows where to walk. I guess she was born knowing that. I can't say the same for my family. We all got bullet holes in our heads and we couldn't even make a go of that because some of us lived.

Take my cousin Spit Boy. Spit Boy was big. He must of been over six feet when he was ten years old and maybe three hundred pounds. He could roll his eyes right back in his head and we said Spit Boy is so full of boogers his eyes are white. I guess he'd spit up about as often as most people take a breath, and he didn't care where he did it. We never heard his mother tell him to cut out the horking and we figured she must of thought he was something kind of special spreading his snot like the fool in the Bighouse.

Spit Boy had this thing for dead animals, like my sister Rose. He gave them funerals in them canoe balers Sassy made from cedar bark. Whatever Rose wasn't nailing to our door, Spit Boy was gathering up and sending down the river. He put them in this nice bed of dry moss and lit fire to them. It was pretty to watch.

67

Soon as the burning boat took off with this little dead animal in it, he stood up and spat. The fire made a hissing noise, but he never did put it out.

Alex said making them balers was a bad thing. Balers got cut from the bark and he said it killed the tree. What kind of crazy Indian thing was that hurting the trees where our late mothers and grandmothers were talking. Between Sassy and Spit Boy there was a lot of them tree trunks with bare places in them.

My sister LaVerne says it's lucky when a bird drops on you. I guess everyone thought Spit Boy was good luck until the time he gobbed on some honky in a bar. That guy didn't believe a mouthful of boogers was a handshake. He put Spit Boy in a wheelchair and he got extra money for that but it didn't make him happy. He couldn't go to the river no more with his canoe balers full of dead animals, so he put his rifle in his mouth and blew his ear off. He missed on account of the wheelchair rolling. He should of put the brake on. I don't know if you'd call it lucky or not.

Maybe it was them cut out parts from trees that made the holes in the fire Ruby was talking about. My mother might of seen the Prince in the fire and then she went looking for him and got lost and fell into one of them black holes. I hear her calling me in the trees and I don't know if she is telling me that is a good place to go or not.

My sister Rose must of heard her too because she took that gun she used to catch all them little animals she nailed on the door and went into the woods with it. She said she was going for a dirt nap and nobody followed her because that killing was her business. When they found her, half her face was gone and the rest was as white and perfect as the Madonna in the church. Whiter. It took a lucky bullet to make my sister white enough to get into heaven.

It sure felt good when I burned the church down.

68

16.
Missing Jesus

I don't know how many of them lettuces I ate that time but they all came five finger discount from the Overwaitea store. I told April and she said "Serves them right!" because she shopped there and they wouldn't let Booger, her littlest kid, use the toilet. The Overwaitea lady said they didn't have one and I told her now you know what it feels like to be an Indian. April got the big boys to chug a couple cokes, then she stood them all in front of the store and told them to pee on the window and they did. I wish I seen it.

It was about the time I started to grow in funny ways. I wasn't too happy about that. My brother Lester was real strong. He worked out with them barbell things. Lester said I should eat spinach like Popeye and then I'd get big like him, but Indians don't eat spinach. In fact, I had a real bad memory of spinach from Father Jim's. I decided I was gonna eat lettuce.

They watch you real good at the Overwaitea. Us Indians got our own special escort service. You could say we were special customers. Hey, but I got moccasins. I discounted one hell of a lot of lettuces. It was sure easier stealing them than eating them. In the end, it didn't make no difference at all. I was still a skinny little runt and I got the runs.

It was April that gave me that pink medicine to take and she laughed about it. She said I was crazy to listen to stuff like that. You had to be strong in your heart.

That was before I went to jail and before they left the farm and went back to the city and got divorced. When I was in jail, I thought a lot about that pink stuff and how much better it tasted than lettuce and how we used to sit at her table and make pictures and smell the food cooking on her wood stove. I wished I told her my secrets, but I never did.

When you tell people things, you put a load on them, like Sister Mary Joseph. All the Indians went to her and every single story was a big stone on her shoulder. She was a real little lady, less than five feet. Sister prayed all the time but that didn't stop her from falling over when the pile got too heavy.

She was always asking Jesus for help, but sometimes Jesus was busy. Maybe she was missing Him the way my mum missed my real father. You can make a pretty good story out of somebody you don't have to live with. It's the same with me. What if I did stay in the palace with them other guys? Maybe they wouldn't like me. Maybe I wouldn't like them. Maybe it's hard being rich and having your picture taken all the time. Look at my father's wife. It killed her, didn't it?

Sister Mary Joseph was drunk at Holy Communion and somebody smelled her breath so they took her to the Mother House. That was the last I seen of her because soon after there wasn't a church no more, thanks to me, and I went to the Indian Hotel.

Like I said, they don't let you see the stars in jail. It isn't one bit like the movies where they bring you beans on a tin plate and you sit and look out the window until some guy comes along with a file and cuts the bars and sets you free so you can ride off in the night together and maybe rob a train full of honkys with watches. There are a lot of Indians in jail and a lot of guys like Father Jim who don't know you in the daytime, but in the dark they are real happy to pretend you're the back end of someone they're missing.

I'll tell you what I did. The first night I cried and the next day this guy said he was gonna take care of me. And he did, but I had to bend over a chair for him. Those guys never see your face. They never say your name.

I just closed my eyes when it happened and I saw stars, lots of them, and I remembered this song Ruby sang that made me think about my mother.

> Over there. Over there.
> I'm gonna wear a starry crown.
> Over there.
> Got no skillet. Got no lid.
> But I'm gonna get my shortenin' bread.
> I'm gonna wear a starry crown.

Over there. To tell the truth, I forgot what my mother looked like. What I could see was the Princess and she had on a blue dress with sparkles and a jewelled crown and she was smiling at me. The sisters told us Jesus said "Suffer the little children to come unto me" and I would of walked a hundred miles in my bare feet just to hear her say my name.

I never did get strong from eating lettuce but I also never let those guys see me cry again and that's something, in'it?

17.
The Super Bowl

This happened not too long ago. Except for Sassy and M'zelle, who didn't know me anyway, I never seen the guys from home. I got my own story now and it's got nothing to do with them. I'm a city person and I hear they live the same old life minus the fishing on account of the fish being brought to the res in a dump truck. Everyone is driving the same cars, except the ones that got totalled, and they wait for the cheques and watch wrestling and football on TV and the kids stay out of the way when there's drinking. That's my family, anyway. Other guys got jobs and pay attention to our culture, but my brothers and sisters are still orphans no matter how many kids they make.

Ever since Donna died, I been staying away from Maison Vay Vay on account of that being the place I met her. I'm a one person Indian and I'm not up for playing peek-a-boo in the nightie rack with any of those old Queens hanging around there.

Every day is Hallowe'en at Vay Vay. You got the ladies with big hands and the pickers and most of them are scarier than a fool in a booger mask. It's no place for poor people anyway, which is why I laughed at what them guys done. Vay Vay gets all the stuff for nothing and then they sell it back for too much money. No wonder so many people do five finger discount in there. Why should poor people pay big money for used clothes when they should be getting them for free?

I know this one girl who sings in a restaurant. All she gets is tips. She sleeps with one of them Vay Vay supervisors and he lets her change all the prices on her dresses. She buys a lot of dresses and sells them to her friends. Everybody on the street knows everybody else's business. It ain't much different from the res.

My late girlfriend had a whole closet full of party dresses. She was the most beautiful person I ever saw. If you didn't get too close, she looked just like a real princess. Anything that had sparkles on it, she liked. "I AM your starry crown, honey" she told me when we got dressed up and went out at night. People stared at Donna. All her clothes came from the Maison. She had an eye, she said. Donna walked down them rows and pounced on fancy silks the way my brothers spotted fish in the river.

"It's like fishing," she said. "You got to be patient."

When Donna got sick, I went looking for nice things to cheer her up. It made her feel good to sit up in bed with her hair and nails done and one of them "new to you" party dresses on. I took a lot of pictures with her camera, but after she died I didn't have the money to get them developed. I just keep them rolls of film in my pocket. She's in there like the tiny lady that lives in the radio and sometimes I hear her whisper in that smokey voice she had.

I went in this one day because it was raining and besides I wanted to smell Donna. When she died, her son turned up from Calgary and he changed the lock on her apartment. I never got to take nothing to keep, excepting my drum and the film. Even my own things got locked up in there.

I wanted to burn some of them party dresses, our way, so she'd have them in her new life. Sometimes when I'm dreaming I see her reaching out of that place. I wish I could put one of them net skirts in her hands, so she could dance up those shiny stairs to heaven. Donna must be real pissed off about leaving her fancy clothes behind her.

So there I was in the nightie section breathing those nightie smells and I hear these voices I know. It's Tom and Auntie Charlene and Lester and LaVerne and most of the kids, I guess. There was lots of them, more than I know the names to. They're mostly heading for the back where they have the furniture, but I seen Auntie Charlene take off her shoes and put on a newer pair. Then she leaves the old ones on the shelf.

The kids all got pop and bags of chips, and there's one holy commotion back there when they're getting themselves chairs and dragging them around. I seen all the cashiers at the front heading like cavalry for the furniture section, but then they retreat because the tills got to be minded.

I call them guys my personal shoppers because they do hang around Indians and they are about the only white guys who see us. So you have to give them credit for that.

I guess they thought Tom and them were going for the big discount and I wonder how they thought a bunch of Indians was going to walk out of Maison Vay Vay with a kitchen set. That would be a table and four chairs. Kind of big for your pockets. I was bigtime curious myself, but I kept my face buried in pink polyester so nobody spotted me.

In case you don't know, you can't see around from the nighties to the furniture, so all I had to go on was a lot of scraping chairs. It sounded like cowboy sex. And then there was the TV's turned up to nine. I come out of my hiding place and peek around that wall with all the kids toys stapled to it and I seen my relatives looking real comfortable in big easy chairs and they're watching the Super Bowl on TV. The little kids are sitting in a sacred circle around another set with cartoons on and they all look real comfortable like it's their own house. They only got one TV at home and so nobody starts a fight they come down and make theirselves at home here. It makes sense to me.

Somebody recognized the top of my head and said "Holy! It's Charlie!" and that was it. Sooner or later they were going to see me like that.

"I'm Charlene too," I said, and all those Indians laughed. I swear they just about wet themselves in them big easy chairs.

18
It Feels Good

In church they say "God be with you" and you answer "And with thy spirit." I started thinking about that. At first, I thought a spirit was a ghost, one of those dead guys who can walk through a wall or talk to you in the middle of the night when no one is there to say if it was true or not, even though you know it was. I seen my mother lots of times that way, especially in the winter time when she went to spirit.

Sister told me it meant the Holy Spirit and you couldn't see that. I thought the Holy Spirit was so full of holes it was invisible, like me. That's what Holy means, I guess. I never told Sister what I was thinking because she would of said it was rude and she'd hold back the sandwiches until I got it right and I didn't want that to happen.

She would of said the only invisible thing about me was when I stood sideways and you couldn't see nothing because I was so skinny. She would of said none of God's children were invisible to Him, because she believed that in her heart. But, if that is true, how come she got so upset and started drinking so

76

much they had to take her away to the nun's rehab centre? If all God's little children were so special to him, how come he let the bad things happen, even in the church, which is s'posed to be God's house? How come they happened to me, eh?

I never told April about Father but she already knew about that kind of stuff. Sister said God was love, one hundred percent, but April got a red face and asked how come little kids got drownded paddling logs away from the love school on Kuper Island? How come kids got hit on the hands with rulers just for speaking our language?

April liked to say "How come" all the time and I guess I learned it from her. Booger started saying "cow hum" and we thought it was funny so we said it too. It was our secret code. She'd say "Cow hum" when Sister Superior asked her to come in and talk about something her kids did, like the time Booger got his peepee caught in his zipper just like I did. Sister Superior wanted to know why Booger wasn't wearing any underpants and April said "Cow hum." I think Sister thought April was crazy, but that was OK by me.

April said Spirit was the fire inside you, the thing that sometimes hurt you and sometimes made you clean and better, like the fire in the Bighouse or the fire when somebody dies. "Smoke signals in Heaven" is what she said and she didn't mean the same Heaven the sisters and Father were trying to get into.

I like that idea.

Fires make the bad stuff go away, like the little schoolhouse we burned on Hallowe'en. When that house goes up in smoke, it feels so good. No more detentions. No more kids calling you names in the hall. No more feeling hungry when other guys are eating lunch. No more sitting in your wet runners and your only pair of Holy jeans thinking three o'clock will never come. No more feeling dumb. No more Father coming around for special lessons.

It started with boxes of matches. I five-fingered them from the store and lit them one at a time. Then I got to lighting the whole box. Then I started piking lighters. They were easier. I filled up my pockets with Bics and I never got caught doing that.

That was a great fire the time my white brothers burned up their toys when April and Alex split up. It was like the whole world was on fire. We torched the Playmobil kids and the pirate ship and the cabbage patch dolls and the Lego castle and cows and horses and fences, everything you could think of. That felt good. In the end we all peed on it and the smell was what made us laugh even harder.

One other time they started the farm gas on fire and that scared the piss out of them because they couldn't put it out and it looked like the whole farm was gonna go up in smoke. Lucky for them it rained buckets. I knew this other honky kid at school who lit his mother's perfume on fire. When she got mad at him for doing that and took him to a shrink, he burned down the house. That learned her, eh?

My first fire, like I said, was at Father's. It was a little fire and I peed on it to put it out. I guess he knew who did it but he didn't say nothing, because he would of got into trouble if I told why. Maybe not though. Who's gonna believe an Indian kid when a priest puts his hand on the Bible?

It got so everytime something pissed me off, I got out my lighter and the gas and stuff I hid in my white brother's tree fort and got to work. I called it my job because somebody had to make them see what people like me feel like inside. I waited 'til night and made like a moccasin Indian. It was real easy. They never caught me for ages, not 'til I was ready.

My fires got bigger and bigger. When they got so big I couldn't put them out by myself, I grabbed a phone and called 911. Then I'd stick around and watch the fire engines come along and put it out. I never set fire to a house except for Father's and I never hurt nobody.

I always had my fires at night and always torched buildings that felt as empty as me. When they had fire coming out of the windows as fast as Sassy running away from Auntie when she was getting ready to beat him, I felt good and warm. It was real beautiful, the flames reaching up into the sky. I hope my mother saw them, even though some people thought it was a bad thing. I know she understood because I got born out of a fire and that was her doing.

The little church by the river was my last fire. It was a good one too. The church was made of wood. I poured gas all over it and lit it and right away it roared and the flames went straight up through the trees. You could hear all them pews and prayer books crackling. What a sound. And the brown wooden Jesus over the altar was growling in a low voice and thanking me because how else was he gonna get down from the white man's cross?

I never called 911 that time. The church was too far from a phone booth and, by the time I came down from getting off on it which was better than any drug I ever tried, there wasn't nothing left. I could hear the river rushing by. I never felt so clean and good up to then. I wasn't even mad at Father then or nobody else neither.

I guess I went to sleep. The next thing I remember, this cop was poking me with his foot and it was morning and all the birds were singing and before you could say "Holy smoke" I was on my way to the Indian Hotel and room service, sardines and toast for breakfast again.

19
Making Babies

I guess those Indians went back to the res and spread the word around they seen me dressed like a girl at Maison VayVay. Before long, Two Dogs One Blanket, who lives down by the apple tree under the bridge that goes up and down, told me Sassy wanted me to meet him on his corner, which is Government and Yates Street. Sassy has his meetings there, right on the street. He likes to show people it's his land and no matter how many times they bust him or take his chair away, he's the boss of that corner.

It's the best corner in town. Lots of people give him money, even when he doesn't play his mouth organ. He told me some white people are going to take a collection and put a statue of him there when he goes to spirit. I seen them wooden Indians before.

Anyways, when I got to Sassy's corner, he's sitting there eating a jumbo bag of french fries with this real well dressed woman who I don't even recognize. I have to rub my eyes to believe it really is Starlene, who I heard worked in the band office and then got herself a job teaching Indians how to make big money doing art.

Starlene said she had a nice apartment and a whole closet full of clothes. She said she got good money from the government and Indians with gold rings and fancy cars. She was gonna take me and Sassy out for a real special lunch, but Sassy had to stay on his corner because some other guy was looking at it. I said no one was gonna take his corner, but he said "No Indian guy." The one who was after it was the black guy who plays trumpet. "He's not in our tribe," Sassy said. "He's a whitecomer." I guess I know what he meant by that.

Sassy is the only elder we got on the street. You got to believe what he says. He's the only old guy that hasn't died yet. There has to be a good reason for that.

Star had this weird haircut. Her hairs looked like one of them purple weeds with prickles on it. She said she got it cut once a month at a beauty parlour. I almost asked her which one. Just in case I got the urge to burn again, I didn't want to cause her no trouble, even though I thought burning was too good for the guy who wrecked her long Indian hairs.

Star was wearing this grey suit with pants and gold earrings with raven carved on them. It's not my taste, but I have to say she looked real smart. I didn't think she'd been shopping at the Maison by the look of her. Besides, I would of seen her.

Starlene said she had this problem. She got everything in the world a girl could want, butcept a baby. I would of thought that was the last thing an Indian girl with nice clothes and a fancy place to live with a dishwasher would be wanting a baby, but she said she had her dreams, and that was that.

I asked her if she got a boyfriend and she said no, she didn't like to be with men. She said she liked girls, and I started thinking our whole family was going to hell in a basket on account of me and her.

"How are you going to get a baby, then?" I asked her.

The sun was shining down on this day and she looked at me with her eyes real narrow and her freckles popping out the way I remember her meaning business, and she said "From you."

I said "No way I'm stealing babies." That would be a one way ticket to the Indian Hotel and they aren't too nice to Indians in dresses in there. She said I got the wrong idea. I was gonna make one with her. I thought "Great! Put two cousins together and you get a baby with two peepers, four bosoms and two baby holes. That's just perfect." I didn't say nothing, because that is my secret. I just said cousins fucking cousins wasn't a good idea. She said she didn't want to do that and besides we were cousin cousins not cousins, that's once removed. She wanted me to do it in a bottle and she'd put it in herself with one of them turkey basters. "Why me?" I asked. "Why not one of those big Indian artists with gold necklaces and German cars."

"You're the best looking," she said. "I want a good looking baby and I don't want no one to know about it. You won't tell. I know you won't because you never did." I figured Starlene was still as crazy as she was when she rode that horse bare-back and jumped over fences. There was something wild about her that all the swell clothes in the world couldn't hide.

"You're crazy," I said. She said never mind crazy and come over to her place when Sassy got his corner covered. We could have anything we wanted for dinner. "Name it," she said.

So we did. She gave me ten bucks and, as soon as Two Dogs and One Blanket came along to babysit the corner, me and Sassy took a cab to this place in James Bay where there is an elevator. We got up to her apartment and it had windows all the way around and a balcony. It was a long way down from that balcony. Sassy said he wouldn't want to be drunk in that place. It gave him the creeps.

Star told us to make ourselves at home. She had this comfy sofa and me and Sassy sat side by side while she got us lemonade from the kitchen. It was real lemonade. "You get lemons," she said, "make lemonade. I'm sending my kid to university."

I was thinking it is a long way from this sofa to university, but I don't say nothing because Starlene and Sassy was talking about steak and potatoes and I hadn't eaten all day on account of my pog running out and a shortage of Johns because it's Easter week-end and they're all at home with their families.

Starlene said she could close the curtains, but I said wait 'til the stars come out. That would be lucky. She liked that idea a lot. Starlene thought of everything. When it got to be dark, she put on this music and lit some candles. I could hear the pans warming up in the kitchen. Pret'soon I'd be smelling them steaks.

"I'm gonna give you a hundred bucks on top of it," she said and then Sassy said he wanted to get into the act too. That would be two hundred dollars. That woman really wanted a baby. She said we could both do it, but she would only be keeping mine and that made Sassy happy.

Starlene gave us two clean jars and went to the kitchen. Me and Sassy sat there in the dark, laughing soft so she wouldn't hear. We made a bet about who was gonna come first. Sassy said it would be him, because he was gonna be sitting at her table with a knife and fork and a napkin around his neck before I could say Geronimo.

I think he was out of practice. I got out my peeper and looked at the stars. I didn't imagine a man and I didn't imagine a lady. I thought about steak. By then I could smell it cooking. It wasn't hard milking my lily. I was used to it, but Sassy had some trouble. I said "Close your eyes and think about Mary and how she used to chase you with a stick," then he came too. I said he still loved her and he said that wasn't it. I made him remember the kloochmas that made her jealous.

Sassy is a joker, you know. He's a raven too. "Starlene is a foolish girl," he said, whispering so she wouldn't hear him over the sound of frying meat. "Let's switch 'em." I said "Mix them up. Some of me and some of you." It would serve her right if her baby got Sassy's big nose. He's got a lot of white in him, enough for a beard. So we did.

Starlene brought us steak and potatoes and a bottle of wine on a tray. "Got any cookies?" I said and Star nearly dropped the tray she was laughing so hard. Me and her both knew she always got what she wanted right from when she was a little kid. She told us to help ourselves to ice cream and then she headed to her bedroom with my jar and a turkey baster. Me and Sassy helped ourselves and then we passed out on her sofa.

In the morning, she said she had to go to work and she gave us each a hundred bucks and a ride downtown. It was a great day for shopping.

20
The End

Ever since I was a little kid, I been running away from home. There was the time I caught a ride to Campbell River and the time I almost got to the United States on the Port Angeles ferry. That time I fell asleep in somebody's trunk. I don't know who it was but it wasn't their fault I was there even though the guy who found me thought I might of been kidnapped, even though I wasn't. The guy driving said "Who'd kidnap an Indian kid anyway? Who'd want him?" His wife just sat there looking mad, her lips pressed tight. Well, he had a point there. They sent me packing on the next ferry and the cop at the other end gave me a teddy bear and brought me back to the res.

I wasn't noticing too many people wanting me, except April, and the band and them weren't too keen on me or any other Indian going in a honky family from what I heard. And I don't think Alex was with her on that one either. He let me drive the hay truck and he took me fishing but I think he thought he already had more than enough kids of his own. That's what April said when she was mad, which was quite a lot. To her mind, there was never too many kids. She didn't like him smoking dope and hanging out with the guys at the river all the time. She thought raising kids was more important than having fun, but then kids were her idea of a good time.

I think the time she lost her finger in the car door was about the end of her and Alex. She stopped playing the piano and she didn't bother getting mad at him no more. Those are bad signs in a woman.

After a while, she started going to the city to read poetry and have tea with ladies. I seen her in high heels and that was a funny sight, eh? My brothers used to sit on the porch and laugh. "She's going to the city to do some talking." All the Indians made jokes about how much April could talk. They laughed, but it gave me kind of a stomach ache because I imagined my own mother going in that direction, even if I don't remember it. I just felt it, eh. It was like catching a big fish and getting it right in your hands and then that sucker just slides right thorough your fingers. You could cry.

One day Alex sold all them sheeps without telling her or nobody and that time she did yell at him. "Those are my babies," she said. "How can you do that?" I think Alex was feeling bad about the foot rot and the lambs the eagles killed in the fields. He was feeling bad about himself too because I think he knew he wasn't really a farmer, after all.

Then there was the time April came back from the city with the kids and found the new pony in the house. It peed on all the rugs and the furniture. Alex must of been down at the river with my brothers. She laughed about that, but Alex told her he didn't want horses either or the dog she gave him for Christmas because it looked sad in the pet store. He already had a dog he liked better, one that didn't pee on the floor every time you patted it because it was glad to see you.

86

Alex was getting rid of everything, even her big bread bowl he sold to this lady in Crofton who didn't want to give it back. I heard April gave her a black eye, but I don't believe it. That was when April must of decided she might as well go too, and the kids with her, but not me. She never said, not me, but I guess she never thought of it either, because she never asked.

One day, this guy came with a truck to take the new pony away. They had to wait for April to come back from the city. Alex and the guy sat on hay bales drinking beer until she comes up and loads the horse on, quiet as can be, which surprised us because before she sweet talked to it that pony was a bucking bronco that wouldn't let nobody take it up the ramp, not me or my white brothers. By the time it was eating hay in the trailer, April was crying so hard, you'd think that horse was her own baby that died the time she liked to talk about when Alex didn't go to the hospital and see her and the kid lying beside her like a blue doll.

So that was that. All the people I love melt like snow on the ground. I can't stop it, eh? The kids had their fire and Alex had a big yard sale and got rid of all the rest of the stuff. Then they sold the farm and all of them went to the city, him too. I call that running away only there weren't no cops to bring them back, even though I wished it a lot of times.

A few times, I caught a ride with my brothers and sisters and went to see them in the big house where Alex and April had different apartments and different friends, but it wasn't the same. I felt like they were different people. For one thing, she didn't smell the same. She smelled like the city. Maybe that's why I came down here later on. I don't know. Anyway, I didn't much feel like going back to the res after I been in jail.

21
Sky Painting
At the Indian Hotel

All them other Indians in jail thought my lettuce story was real funny. No wonder you got into trouble they told me. It was from eating lettuce. Indians don't eat lettuce. The other thing is one smart mouth guy started calling me Dugong, which got me worried because I thought he might be in on one of my secrets. I learned some French at school and I thought he meant "deux gongs", which was sort of true, but he didn't. That Indian must of been looking out the window in French class.

The other guys liked the sound of it, so they all started calling me Dugong. I found out that could of been my Indian name when somebody looked it up in one of them books they have on that book cart that comes around, and it turns out dugong means sea cow that eats five hundred pounds of lettuce a day when they catch it and put it in a zoo.

The Indian Hotel is a zoo too, too many guys with the sky taken away from them. It makes you crazy. The food is pret' bad.

They haven't figured out Indians don't like to eat mystery meat day in day out. You never know what it is. Some guys make a joke of guessing what it might of been to start with, like maybe the warden's cat or them pigeons that shit all over the place. Sometimes you could just cry all day long but you can't because you don't want them to know how much you miss your sky and your river and your fish that you got to know like brothers.

They got this phone in the day room and as soon as you get on some guy is trying to get you off it because he's gotta talk to his old lady or his kids and he says he's gonna whack you if you don't put it down. I couldn't call my sisters and brothers because they didn't have money and the only one I could think of was April. I must of called her a hundred times a day. Not that much, but I just needed to talk to somebody every minute. Once I got beat up for cutting in the phone line.

April just had this operation and she couldn't come and visit, but she always answered the phone. She said it was next to her bed and her new room was white. Everything white. "My life is a blank canvas" she said. She was starting over. I wished I could too. I wished I was Onegong and I couldn't remember nothing bad that happened, except for my mother going to spirit, which was beautiful because seeing her go up in the sky in her blanket of snow is the only time I remember her.

April and me talked about the good things. We laughed about the raisins and the wedding party and she told me bad things my white brothers were up to like unscrewing the Christmas lights at the government because of what they were doing to our trees. I told her about saving up all the fruit salad and putting it in plastic bags. We drank it on Saturday night after the movie and got pretty high, eh.

In the Indian Hotel you got to get through every day one at a time. You just got to eat the food and try to sleep and not think too much about how you screwed up or who screwed you. April said she was looking at her white wall and seeing me ride across it on the new pony. I said that was a nice picture and I wished I could paint some so she promised to get the prison guys to let me have some paints and papers 'cause that is one of the things I like to do the best.

And she did. It took a long time because nobody's gonna do you a big favour when you got a red suit and a number instead of a name and a life but she got the Big Indian Honchos to get on their case and I got my things to paint with. I had to do it in front of the guard in the day room in case I thought of putting my paint brush where the sun don't shine or into some other loser, but that was O.K. by me. At lock-up time, I closed my eyes and thought up the pictures and they were all ready in my mind, so I just had to put them down when I could.

The other guys thought they were real nice. Pret' soon everyone had my pictures in their houses, which is what we called our cells. They traded me their tuck stuff, lots of chocolate bars, and some guys gave me drugs, especially the guy that was looking after me.

I sent April a picture of her in her nightiegown and her rubber boots the night she took off on her bicycle. She said she put it on her wall and it made her laugh every time she looked at it. It didn't hurt her to laugh no more.

When I was making them pictures, I was happy. I didn't know I was in jail. I was free, swimming in the river or running through the woods to visit my white brothers or lying on my back looking up at my mother who was all white and fluffy in the sky. I put the pictures of her right on the ceiling of my house so I could see her when I was on my bed.

I don't know what happened to all them pictures. I left them when they let me out. I sure hope the next guy liked them.

22
Street Time

No one says street time's good time, but it's better than jail. I could go walking down the road and never get to the end, not 'til it turned into the sea and there is no end to the sea. Sometimes I've thought I could start swimming and see how far I got, maybe no place, but that would be O.K. too. I could visit my brothers, the salmon people.

Lots of guys on the street go to spirit. Some of them O.D. and some of them just lie down and go to sleep. Not very many people see us guys, don't matter if we are Indians or not. They just step over us like we're a bump on the sidewalk. You got your hand out and you're not so clean, they don't want to look at your face, which is sometimes dirty and sometimes beat up.

I take care of myself. You got some washrooms you can go to and get fixed. You got to be fast, that's all, before somebody with a nice house with a bathtub who wouldn't shake hands with you tells you to move along. I know how to avoid them type of people. So long as I look OK, some guy's gonna pay me for catechism lessons. That's what I call it. Protein floats, holy wafers, whatever. It's better for me to do a job and get paid than ask for money. Asking for money sucks bigtime, bigger than the other thing.

I got my friends. We look out for each other. You just got to remember who gets what place to sleep and who gets to panhandle on what corner. Otherwise some guy's gonna turn your face into dogfood.

Sometimes I stand on the same corner all day waiting for April to come by, but I never seen her. She's busy writing her books now, I guess. I never talked to her since jail. I phoned her up and didn't say nothing a coupla times. She got the hang of it and she said "Charlie, is that you? Are you OK?" but I kept quiet. I don't know why. I guess I didn't want to make her feel bad.

She already knows about Sassy 'cause he told me she went to the city to give them hell for letting the store people take away his chair. Sassy said talky women come in handy sometimes because he got his chair back, only somebody took it away again.

I would 'specially tell her about Mabel, who is a girl dressed like a man. She must be three hundred pounds. I never saw anyone so big as Mabel. All I can say is she's no lettuce eating Dugong. Mabel hangs around bakeries and snitches bread when they leave the back door open. Lucky for her bakeries is hot. She is one strong woman. I seen her arm wrestle real big guys and never get beat. One chief came down here in his big Mercedes car and took her on. You should of seen the look on his face. We all wanted her to win 'cause she's one of us, even though the big car chiefs make us proud to be Indians.

Mabel don't say nothing, but she's teamed up with Marie, this little tiny lady whose legs don't work. Marie does all the talking for both of them. She had herself a wheelchair to start with, but someone stole it while she was sleeping and now Mabel carries her everywhere. It's a pret'sight those two women helping

THE MEMOIRS OF CHARLIE LOUIE

each other out. I don't see no honkys carrying each other around like that. It makes me think of me and Donna.

The street is not so bad, not as good as living in a nice place with someone to cuddle up in bed with and talk to, but I got friends and we help each other as much as we can. Mostly I keep myself clean and pick up a little money. I signed up at the hostel and I get a little pog that way, but I never go there except to get the money because there's too many rules.

Sometimes a guy asks me out for a meal or over to his place, but I'm afraid of doing that because some guys turn mean and I don't need a broken face. The street is not my real home. It is the place I am now. My real home is where I am going next. I seen pictures of my real father in his stone house with all them hard chairs. Maybe he's got to keep going too. Maybe he likes to look up. The sky belongs to him and me and everybody. That's a better roof than any other one I seen.

23.
Orphans

"You're so pretty," April said. "You could be a girl." There's one thing, and that's my ears. My ears are big enough to hold a crown up. When me and the kids played dress-up, I got to be queen. Mostly we played The Pope and Chinese Emperor. I liked Chinese Emperor best because of the green tea and the cakes with plum sauce inside. I like my hairs long because they cover my ears. I never think of cutting my hairs and selling them, not even when my welfare's gone.

When Donna got sick and the medicine made her hairs fall out, I told her "I'm gonna cut mine too" so we can be the same and she said no because she liked touching mine. She said they sang like the hairs in a violin bow.

April played violin and piano too. All her boys played something. One day she took a bunch of us kids roller skating in town and somebody shut the door on her finger when she turned around to see if it was locked. Her finger came right off and there was blood spurting out of the end of it like those oil wells I seen on The Beverly Hillbillies. "One of you's got to drive," she said.

94

"Charlie, you got to." That's on account of I drove the hay wagon around the farm, but this was different. This was on the road, man, and I was scared shitless. All the kids were crying in the back seat and here's April holding her hand out the car window because she doesn't want to get the inside bloody and her face looks like a ghost.

I got her to emergency and they sewed that finger back on. The nurse made me get it out of the door, because I was the oldest. I put her finger in this bowl of bad smelling stuff and they gave it back to her. We said she was a starfish. Alex didn't want to come to get her at the hospital because he was putting the sheep through the foot bath, but he did.

I didn't hear her play any songs after that. She was pretty mad at Alex. She said she was always mad at Alex since her baby died, which I don't remember because I was a baby too. He didn't want to come and get her then neither, she said.

I got to drive the car one other time. When the hay was in, Alex went to Vancouver and he asked me to deliver some meat for him. I said OK and took my little cousins for a ride first. That was a great day. We went down to pebble beach and had some bologna sandwiches and pop and then we drove around. It sure was hot. The kids rolled down the windows and stuck their heads out like dogs do. Pret'soon we ran out of gas.

It was lucky my Auntie Charlene came by in her pick-up and we caught a ride back to the res. By then I forgot about the delivery.

The load was two lambs Alex butchered before he went away. Boy did that car smell bad when he got it back. April said it would be a good idea if I stayed away for a few days until he cooled down.

He was about as mad as that time we jumped off the barn in our king clothes. That wasn't my idea. It was Gabe's. He wasn't scared of nothing. He said if we jumped our capes would help us fly. Then he said, you go first. I did and I landed in a pile of straw and manure and that wasn't too bad, but Gabe missed and he broke his ankle. He got a lot of presents and we drew pictures on his cast, but Alex said it was just a way of getting out of his chores.

When you're there, it's just life, but when you think about it, some things were real fun. When we rolled up comics and smoked them, we got sick and it didn't feel too good, but now I have to laugh about that.

One time I was over there, the kids had this pumpkin. Gabe got a knife and cut a hole in it. He said this is how you got a baby and he stuck his John Henry in and out of there. I just watched. I already seen how you got a baby and it wasn't with pumpkins, that's for sure. They said it felt good and I almost said they should take one to Father Jim, but I didn't.

We watched the pigs fucking and the sheep fucking and the cows fucking. Everything was fucking on that farm. I felt sorry for the cats. The cats don't like it one bit. I heard a cat has a John Henry like a barbed wire fence. I been caught on one of those more times then I want to tell you and I wouldn't want it inside of me. That's for sure.

They ate the pigs and the lambs and the cows, but they didn't eat the cats even though I heard some guys did and they got chopped up in the burgers down at the Ding Ho Drive-in. Nobody knew what to do with the farm cats. There was too many of them. Some of them lived in the barn and some of them lived in the house. One day April turned on her clothes dryer when a kitty was taking a nap in there. Her sheets came out all bloody and it was Booger's favourite kitten, which was called Booger Junior because it looked like a Booger and Booger got his name because he always had his finger in his nose.

We didn't like what Alex did with his burlap sack, so us kids got this game going. When people came to visit from the city, we showed their kids the new kittens. The city kids all wanted one and we knew their parents were going to say no, so we kept them real busy until the last minute. When they got in their cars to go home, the fathers leaned out the window and asked how long 'til the next ferry. You could bet on that. Then we said, fort-five minutes, and that is about how long it takes to drive there. Those guys would gun it and get out of there in a big cloud of dust. The surprise was their kids had already rolled down the windows in the back seat. We just threw them kittens in and away they went. By the time the guys in the front seat heard them, it was too late to turn around.

It sure beats drowning kittens.

I wish the kids had done that to me. I might of liked growing up in a city house with steak for dinner every night.

24.
The Visit

It's funny what you remember about people. Rose smelled like bleach. Sister smelled like church wine. So did my dad. April smelled like bread. M'zelle had these golden hairs on her arms. When I think about Seattle Ruby, I can't see her face but I remember the songs. I know the words to all of them. Sister said you remember stuff when you don't know nothing. My brothers smelled like fish. The first Charlene who was married to my cousin Tom had fat hands. I see them full of berries. Tom said she picked berries like the devil was chasing her. If you ask me, the devil is always hungry.

When I was in jail, I tried to remember that one thing about everyone I ever knew. Father Jim sounded like he had rocks in his mouth. Sometimes I made up that the stones been in the sweat lodge fire and they burned him. I always was scared of his mouth. I can still see it up close with food in it. He has his lips open and it looks like a laundrymat in there. Donna used to be a dentist. She said dentists go crazy looking in people's mouths. They blow their brains out just about as much as Indians do.

Sister said the mouth is the door to the soul because you swallow Jesus. I guess that's what happened to her. She got thirsty for Jesus, just like Father Jim. If you could only forget to swallow or breathe when he put himself in your mouth, you wouldn't choke like that. I learned about that.

The guards smelled like gum. My mother smelled like smoke. She been in the fire and she pulled me out of it, I figure, only I fell in again. Prison was bad. There was a phone in the day room. My brothers and sisters got no phone. The Sisters got a phone, but they wouldn't let me call collect. I phoned April, sometimes ten, twenty times a day. She sent me paper and paints and letters and they didn't smell like bread. It drove me crazy. I wanted to smell her over the phone, but I couldn't. When I got out, nothing smelled the same. My brothers and sisters finally got a new house.

The time I ran away to the city, I slept in a field. It was one of those nights with shooting stars. I lay down on my back and looked up at the sky and I tried to see my mother's face, but I couldn't. I was real cold. I got together some sticks and grass and lit them on fire. I made my wish, then I touched my tits and both places between my legs, what the guys at school called the Holy Three, to see if any of them went away, but they didn't. When I was warm enough, I shut my two-coloured eyes and went to sleep.

I dreamed the Princess was dancing in the sky. She was wearing a diamond crown and a silver dress with silver shoes. Her skirt was full of stars. When I woke up, it was still dark. I smelled smoke. I could hear something. It was eating.

I had another match, so I lit it. The sky was full of stars and the field was full of people. They were pale as the ghosts of white people and they stood perfectly still.

In the morning, the grass was all eaten down. When I told Donna about it, she said it was a visit from the Lambs of God.

Donna smelled like funerals.

25.
Dressed To Kill

In the city, I dress to kill. That's what Donna said. Even though I got two different eyes and some skin-heads knocked out my front teeth one night in fag forest, I still look pretty when I dress up. I just got to remember not to smile.

That is one reason why M'zelle didn't know me that time in front of the Bishop's place across the street from the parkade where she jumped.

When I went to the city, I found out guys got paid for doing what Father Jim got for free. I did pretty good, because I got customers both ways and they all wanted the same thing. The guys thought I was a girl and the other guys paid extra for getting a girl with a dick. Ten bucks for five minutes, maybe ten, and all the time I was pretending I was a princess in my castle dresses.

I never had my own place, but I got a big suitcase at Maison Vay Vay and I kept my dresses in it and my blanket and money and the free baggies I got from the street nurse. It was hard to walk in high heels and carry my suitcase, so I helped myself to a cart from Thrifty's. Then I got a dog from a guy who O.D.'d. The other kids on the street called him Sitting Bull because he had a mean face and nobody ever got to steal nothing from my cart.

That was before I met up with Donna.

I actually seen her before I met her. She lined up with them pickers at the Maison first thing every morning. Donna looked like she came out of a magazine. She wore these big hats and dresses with full skirts and really high heels that made her way taller than me. Even before she got sick, her hairs were short. She had a pattern cut in them that she called tweed. It was kind of a zigzag. I liked the way they felt when you touched them.

She bought so many dresses, but I never said nothing to her and she never said nothing to me until the time I was changing a pair of old high heels for some new ones and she offered to pay. I said OK and one thing led to another. After that, I had my own place and a red Studebaker to drive around in, but I had to give away Sitting Bull because they wouldn't let dogs in the apartment.

I gave him to another junkie who let him get run over.

Donna was rich, but not as rich as the people who give their dresses to the Maison. Some of them dresses cost as much as a car and those people would wear them one time, maybe two and then give them away. A lot of them was brand new with the price tags still on them. I got to know which ones were better. You can tell by the cloth. Donna had a real good eye for dresses.

The first time I went home with her she made a bubble bath and washed my back for me. No one ever did that before. I was so happy I cried. She made me feel like a real princess not a pretend one. We helped each other with our make-up and acted like sisters. We kissed the air and said I love you and that was all except for lying side by side in bed. Donna liked to sleep with my tits in her hands. I miss that.

After she died and her son locked me out of our apartment, I never got my dresses back, but I didn't care no more. That part of my life was over. I started dressing like a guy again and now I just live on my pog and some panhandling. All I got is my drum. I don't even own a suitcase. Since Donna's gone and the Princess's gone and Sitting Bull's gone, I didn't see the point of dressing up no more. Castles aren't what they're cracked up to be, if you ask me.

I never knew rich people before I went to the city. Some Indians got big cars on account of selling art, but I never got to ride in one of those. I been in some fancy cars since I left the res, some of them all done up like a coffin inside. That's what I figured out. We're all heading to the same place. The only choice you got in life is when you go there.

Donna got to choose in the end.

I guess she also chose what she got because she was smart enough to know smoking was bad for her. I never said nothing about it but I never started up neither. For one thing, cigarettes cost money, unless you pike them.

She always had this funny throat and then one day when we were driving along in the Studebaker she started to cough and she covered her mouth with her glove and her glove had blood on it. I seen that before and I thought she had TB which some guys on the res got, but it wasn't.

"Don't let me get ugly," she kept saying, and, when the time came, I got some China White from this guy I know.

First I washed her with water and powdered her all over. I never seen her naked before, but she let me. I filed her nails and painted them red. I made her face beautiful, so you couldn't see the hurting in it. Then I got out the pink Oscar de la Renta gown with the red satin roses. It was her favourite dress and she had shoes to match. I put on her long white gloves with pearl buttons and her pearl earrings.

102

Donna looked beautiful. I made tea and those little sandwiches with no crusts she liked. It was hard for me to think of people cutting off the best part of the bread and throwing it away, but Donna gave them to the seagulls. I put the crusts on the windowsill. Then I put on my white gloves. She was waiting for me to bring in the silver tray. "I'm eating for two," I said, and Donna laughed. She couldn't swallow. I put a slice of lemon in her mouth and she sucked it.

She asked for a record. It was Liberace. Donna liked piano music.

When I gave her the China White, she smiled and said the eleven months she spent with me was the best time in her life, even the sick time. She said she was floating and the clouds were pink and she asked me to finish the story I was telling her. I lay down beside her and held on to one of her white hands. I could feel her heart in it until it stopped.

After a while I kissed her on the mouth. It was the first time. I fixed the bed and phoned her son like she asked me and he came over from Calgary. He never seen her dressed like that before.

26.
What Raven Did

One time in summer, Donna took me to an old house for tea. I never been in a place like that before. I been in cafes for hamburgers and fries and I been in some bars but that was it. On account of I don't have any hairs on my face and my chest parts are real I look like my own sisters. They are real lookers. When Donna started up that chemo, her hairs all came out, but before that she had to shave two or three times a day.

On the tea day, we put on big hats and silk dresses and high heeled shoes. It was hard playing croquet in them. We laughed our heads off, just like me and M'zelle used to. I played croquet on the farm but the ground was bumpy. This tea place had a real honky lawn. Donna said it was as smooth as a baby's bum, and I laughed so hard I got lipstick on my teeth. She said I was good at this game but the fact is I am good at lots of games. I never tried polo though. I seen him do it on the news.

I would like to ride a pony like that and win a silver cup. My father would be real proud of me. Indians and princes all like horses. That is one thing we got in common. That's for sure.

I did beat Donna at this croquet game and she pouted a little bit, but that was OK by me. She was paying. The tea, which was one sandwich cut in four pieces and one lemon tart and one piece of thin cake and one cookie each, came to thirty dollars. That could feed my brothers and sisters for a week, if you count that the fish we eat at home is free.

It was the most fancy sandwich I ever seen, three layers with different kind of bread and different food in the middle. One was eggs and one was cucumbers. I remember that. At the farm, we made animal sandwiches with the cookie cutters. That was fun. I liked the honey bunnies most. Them tea sandwiches were so pretty, it was hard to eat them. Of course I did. I even licked my fingers. Donna said that was rude, but if I left my gloves on they would of got food on them, that would of been ruder.

This Chinese guy brought us tea on a silver tray. He walked like a crow. He said his grandfather worked in the old house in the olden days. His grandfather didn't speak the white people's language and he was so lonely for home he went out to the barn and sang his songs to the cow that gave them their milk. You can still hear the singing sometimes, he said. That made me feel real sad.

There we were sitting on this honky grass looking at the water and acting like white people and there was the ghost of this unhappy grandfather hanging around.

He told us this other story about how the grandfather got famous. There was this picnic on the day honkys celebrate their country which is really our country and they left the grandfather at home with the animals. The honkys were taking picnics across the wooden bridge to a park on the other side. There was horses and buggies and people walking and this trolley car going on wires and the grandfather was looking over and thinking there was too many white people on the bridge and he was right.

Right in front of his eyes, the bridge started to swing back and forth, and then it came down with all the people on it. He said there was screaming and drowning, with horses and buggies and babies all mixed up in the water and the people in the trolley car never got out at all. They was trapped in there and lots of them drownded without even a chance at getting saved.

Lucky there was boats there that helped some of them get out of the water, but those trolley car folks was trapped. There was no air to breathe in there. They overloaded the car for this holiday and that was why it happened.

This Chinese guy's grandfather couldn't swim, but he took all the curtains down and he ran to the edge of the water and wrapped up the people that got saved and later he made them tea. They said he was a hero because he did the right thing, but he still had to eat in the kitchen after that.

So here I was drinking tea in a white chair on the white people's lawn with my little pinkie up in the air and nobody told me to eat in the kitchen. The sun was shining on my face and I was feeling about as good as it gets when I heard Raven making a gulping sound like ladies drinking tea. He was laughing at two men dressed like women making women sounds and that was OK. I figure that is how we all get to be one like they tell you at church. Sometimes I think God is a black bird that can make any noise he wants to.

27.
Good News

One day I'm downtown getting medicine and I stop to talk to Sassy. He says he has news for me and it's from Starlene. I never forgot about that time me and Sassy went to her place, but, to tell you the truth, I never believed the turkey baster would of worked, especially after we stirred up our jars.

Sassy reaches real slow into the pocket where he keeps his harmonica and his medicine bag and gets out this picture of a baby girl. He smiles real big. "It's ours," and he laughs so hard tears come down his face.

The baby girl is dressed up fancy and she has a bow in her hair. "Starlene says she is real smart. She's walking and talking already and she's got ten fingers and toes." I never asked him about nothing else. I figure that's Star's business.

I had some money left over from picking up Donna's medicine, so I bought me and Sassy a cigar each and we sat there on this corner smoking them and laughing like two real live cigar store Indians. It made me laugh to think those honkys driving by in their car wouldn't believe the Indian guy in the dress and the old Indian guy with crutches were celebrating their baby daughter. "What's her name," I asked him. He said "Hope." That Starlene never did give up on an idea once she got it in her head. Maybe our daughter will go to university.

28.
The Time That Midget
Got a Look At Donna's Ass

There is this person called Fire Woman and she can dance and throw burning sticks in the air at the same time. It makes me remember my Auntie who chased her husband with a stick from the fire when he put his eyes on other women. You would never fool around on Fire Woman. She is more than six feet tall and she goes to the gym to work out. I guess that there fire pay is under the table money.

Donna said she was swallowing fire when she got sick. Father Jim used to say it was a good thing. If you swallowed pain, it made your voice stronger in the end. Maybe that is true, but it wasn't no excuse for what he did to me and all those other little kids. Whoever said your mouth is a church door shouldn't of put his peeper in it. Not when you are a little kid.

I said to Donna, it's OK. Every bit of hurt is a knock on the door to heaven. I had my fingers crossed, 'cause I don't believe any of that stuff no more, but Donna did and she had a picture of

Jesus tattooed on her butt before she changed her mind.

I guess a tattoo is about the only thing that lasts longer than you want it to these days.

That's what them clowns saw when they dragged her into that circus truck that time and took off her clothes. Donna liked the circus. She wanted to be the girl on the flying trapeze, even though she was so scared of heights she couldn't get up on a stepladder to change a light bulb. I said how were you going to go up there and do somersaults without a net if you can't even pee standing up?

What do you think, one night she got in her high heels and she went by herself. I wanted to go hustle a bit of cash anyways. It was gonna be Donna's birthday and I had to go get her something with my own money. I had the idea of taking her for a picnic at the beach with chicken and wine and giving her some real nice earrings. I said I wasn't feeling so good that night even though she had two tickets to the circus and since she had that I'm going anyway look in her eye I knew I was free for an evening of protein floats.

When me and M'zelle were kids, guys drove by the res real slow and took a look at her. Later it happened to me. If the guys don't like you, they speed up and leave rubber on the street. They get real mad if they figure out you are a guy. Some people I know got hurt bad that way, myself included. I had my teeth bust out a couple of times. The worst time was in the bar that time the guy made fun of my picture book, but I don't want to talk about that.

It was like that when Donna went to the circus. She was walking away from the fairground and this van full of clowns pulled up beside her. They was all midgets talking real sweet about Donna being so good looking and they bet she'd be fine on a highwire. That type of thing. Before she knew what happened to her, they had the back door open and her lying down in the van

110

with her skirt pulled up and a midget with a knife sitting on top of her. She could smell dope and that roses room spray that comes in the pink can. The other midgets were laughing about who was gonna get which end of her and the one with a knife cut up her underpants.

I heard about garlic scaring off vampires, but I didn't know you could fix a bunch of midgets with a picture of Jesus tattooed on your ass. Those were the very same midgets that made the kids laugh in the big tent about a minute before.

Donna said it was lucky she was lying on her stomach. She said she was so scared her hands went cold as the water in the Chemainus River after the salmon run. If they had of seen the rest of her, she would of been a goner.

She was anyway. Donna put the wrong thing in her mouth for years and years. When she was a dentist, she said she should have had the franchise for mouthwash. She said her sickness was retribution and I said it was cigarettes.

That night the sitting down midget made a X on her ass so he wouldn't look like such a cracker, and then he told the others to let her go, which they did with only two scratches on her. I would of said she was lucky and she did thank her lucky stars and especially Jesus but that was too soon because she already had a sore in her mouth.

29.
Sometimes Death Comes

Sometimes death comes at night like the guys that grab you and take you to the Bighouse where you find out the ways of my people. The elders learn you the songs and the dances. Something good comes out of that. I seen it many times. People that had a problem with drinking or just being angry with everyone come out feeling good about theirselves.

Some people don't like it. They don't want to spend a winter in there eating Indian food and going to the river four times every day, when it's so cold you have to break the ice to get in the water. I done that after being in the sweat lodge. I don't mind the ice much, but them dead salmon sure feel strange when you step on them.

I got busted once in the middle of the night. I was sleeping in my blanket down by the apple tree and these cops shone their light right on my face. Now I know how the deers feel when they get shot by pit-lampers. I know how Donna felt. It's like some guy wants to get inside you and it don't feel right but you can't stop it.

I never got grabbed and taken to the elders. Maybe I would

of liked it, but there was never enough money in my family to pay for a dance for me. My brothers and sisters were still saving for my late parents' picture dance. You got to feed so many people and give them things. That's hundreds of blankets and oranges and more money than I ever had in my life, even if you added up all my Indian money, which I always get because my sister collects it for me back home because I don't have no address myself.

Starlene learned me all the family stuff after she come out. Her family gave a real good dance for her on account of the carving her brothers sold and the hundreds of sweaters her sisters knit, just for her. Starlene was like a wild horse before she went in, but she came out all serious. Now she's a serious Indian. She's gonna send our daughter to university. She's gonna take care of her when she's sick, like I took care of Donna.

I learned that from April.

The band said I couldn't live at her house, but she let me sometimes. Sometimes I had to run. I didn't know where, but I just took off and kept on until I couldn't go anymore. I had to lie down and go to sleep. Once I got all the way to Campbell River, and I was only six years old.

This one night, I woke up and there was a stranger on top of me. It was taking my breath away. I fought as hard as I could and I got it off, but I was afraid to lie down again. I had this bad cold in my chest.

I took off in the dark and I ran real fast down the railroad track and through the bushes to the farm. It was dark in the house, but the door was open, so I went upstairs. It was real quiet except for the clocks and someone snoring. April was asleep. I saw her face in the moonlight. She was having a good dream because she was smiling. She and Alex were in bed with that kitty whose mother got hit by the train.

April told me she knew it happened because she woke up one morning and the kitty was sucking her breast. I wish I seen that.

I stood and looked at April for a long time. I tried not to cough and that made me want to. My head was hot and I wanted to lie down beside her, but I was scared to. Pret'soon she opened her eyes. I guess I looked like a ghost. She sure looked like she seen one.

I don't know why, but I started to cry and April got up and took the cover off her bed and she wrapped me up in it. We sat in a chair all that night long. I must of been heavy on her. I guess I was ten years old. She held on to me and didn't make me lie down because I was still scared to.

She sang that song I like about the fairies and I still remember the words.

White coral bells
Upon a slender stalk.
Lily of the valley
Deck our garden walk.
Oh, don't you wish
That you could hear them ring.
That can only happen
When the fairies sing.

I used to think it was dumb the way honkys spend so much time growing things you can't eat, but it made sense to me when she learned me that song. When I see flowers now I always stop and listen.

In my culture, you gotta have a song. That's one of the main things you get from your family. It might be your grandfather's song that goes with his name and his dance and you get to keep it too.

Other things got their own song. The flowers gott'em the leaves gott'em, the whales gott'em. The whale song is like radar. That is something I learned from Sister. April told me the sheeps were baaing all the time so the mothers and babies could find each other. I hope my mother will find me when I beat the drum the way I remember from the Bighouse.

Seattle Ruby told me the songs from the slave part of her family was about freedom. Her folks fooled those boss guys that made them sing in the cotton fields so they could tell if they was takin' a nap or gone fishing or maybe gone to our place up here, which is what they did. Some folks was singing and some folks was running away and they are telling each other about it in the songs and having a joke on the guys with the big sticks to beat them with if they didn't work hard enough.

I been thinking a lot about freedom. Some guys in the Indian hotel said freedom was goin' to jail. They didn't want to worry 'bout finding somethin' to eat and a place to sleep where nobody was gonna beat you up and take your bedroll. Others guys go free when they smoke up. Some of my brothers and sisters took bullets to freedom. When I was a little kid, I just took off. I didn't know where I was going, but I always hoped it would turn out good and I would see my mum.

One time I met this one guy who lost his legs in Vietnam. He was a cousin of Seattle Ruby's and he liked dope too. He got busted in the army and sent to jail and they forget to unlock him when the sky started coming down on them. That's how his legs got blown off.

He told me all he ever thought about after that was feeling sand between his toes was his idea of freedom. Once he five fingered every crab in the tank at a fish store and took off the elastics on their claws that stopped them from pinching people that were gonna eat them. Then he took them crabs to the beach and let them go.

I never heard a crab singing, but I bet they were all running down that beach calling for their mothers. That must of made the shoeless guy feel real great.

30.
The Waterfall

When She was sick, I washed her face with a cloth and I put ice into her mouth. It was the only thing she could swallow. Just a little water, and I tried to think of myself as a real small naked person sitting on her tongue and the ice melting was a waterfall full of beautiful colours.

She liked me to tell her stories. I called it the magic canoe. When we got in we could paddle to anyplace we could think of. I took her on a boat way out where my people used to go whale hunting. Sometimes she thought of things like what we had in our picnic basket or what the sun looked like when it went down over the sea.

We went all the way to London where my real father lives. That took us a whole week. Donna and me took turns paddling. We went down around that big canal there and through them islands in the Caribbean and across the Atlantic Ocean. There was lots of whales in that ocean and they played around the boat, but they never upset us. We saw icebergs and ships that looked like a thousand stars at night. There were storms too. Big ones. But we paddled hard and it worked.

When we got to London, England, we passed under the bridge and my real father was there waiting to greet us with lots of other chiefs, but not the Princess. My real father was wearing a golden crown and this big button blanket with fur around the edge. Me and Donna got out in our high heels and it was pretty funny getting our land legs back after all that time in a canoe. After all the speeches and the gifts, they took us in a coach with horses through the streets and all them English people cheered.

My real father and his family treated us good. The Princess asked us over to stay at her palace too and she gave us some of her dresses to wear. We tried on all her jewels and she showed us how she put on her make-up so she looked beautiful all the time. She called it warpaint. I didn't make that up.

The Princess liked dancing, so I taught her my grandmother's dance and she did it good. You should of seen her in her bare feet in the palace dancing around her grand piano like it was a fire in the bighouse. I fell in love with her because she was sad like my mother used to be before she went to spirit. Her feet were big.

That was Donna's favourite story. She made me tell it again and again and every time it got better. We knew the Princess's dresses by heart, because we seen them in so many magazines.

I was telling her that story when she died. We were right in the middle at the part where she is trying on the Princess's shoes and they fit. Donna was smiling and I knew the pain was all gone away.

Sometimes I close my eyes and open my mouth and something happens. I can taste the rain or a nice surprise like food I never had before. In my life, bad things happened in my mouth, like the dentist pulling my teeth when they went bad or somebody half way knocked them out. Or Father.

"Think about the host," he said, and that was about the time God died for me.

Like I said, Donna used to be a dentist, but she said to me "The tooth fairy is coming. Open your mouth and close your eyes." I had a hard time closing my eyes because I was worried, but she made me and I got to taste all those beautiful things. There was fruit I never had before and fancy chocolates and ice cream. There was champagne with bubbles in it that made me sneeze. I can't even remember them all.

What I did for her was putting my whole self in her ear, one naked Indian, half boy half girl, and a waterfall full of shining colours. She said my stories were the best present she ever had, and I believed her.

31.
Don

The worst thing that happened to me when Donna died was not when her son kicked me out of the house. I don't blame him. I guess it would be pret' strange to go check out your dad's place and find all them dresses and an Indian in the cupboard too, eh? I got to thinking the last time he seen Donna she was Don. I tried to imagine about how I would feel about that if it was my dad and I couldn't. I couldn't picture my real dad in a dress and my Indian dad wouldn't of looked so good either. At least my Indian dad didn't have hair on his face, like white men.

The hardest part was when I found a quarter in that phone booth down there on Fisgard Street and I called up just to tell Donna's son I was sorry and maybe he'd like to know what a nice person Donna was and we didn't mean no disrespect to him. We just were what we were.

He didn't answer the phone and I got the message on the answering machine. It was Donna, and she said she'd call me right back and I wished it was true. It was like her voice blew a hole in my head bigger'n any hole my brothers and sisters made in themselves with the .22, that's for sure.

I stood there in that phone booth and cried until the phone fell out of my hand and there was a guy there waiting anyhow who was getting mad at me and I guess he figured he had a real beef, because what right does an Indian have to stand in a phone booth and cry all day long.

None, I guess. You can't buy much for twenty-five cents these days and it might have been his quarter anyways.

Seattle Ruby, my cousin Alfred's wife, sang us this song about a guy who made a banjo out of the back skin of his dead wife. She said he played it like he was making love to her and he expected she could hear him. That's what gave me the idea.

I think if you make a sound that comes from the heart, the right people hear it. Donna must of heard me on the phone that time. I believe that.

I'm gonna catch a ride to the mountain my real father is coming to visit and I know he's gonna hear me, because I'm gonna beat my drum as loud as I can and sing my song and then everyone will know because the TV guys will be there and they will see him turn to look at me and he will see my one blue eye and my big ears and he will know who I am. He will say my name and the whole world will hear him, eh.

32.
Fire On the Mountain

Naming things is real important to my people. You don't even get your Indian name until something happens that makes you real. There was that guy I heard about called Two Dogs Fucking. Don't ask me how he got that one. My Indian name should of been The One His Mother Got Out of the Fire. Something had to keep me warm all that cold night long, eh? Something kept me alive. She must of loved me enough to do that.

I would of done that for Donna even though Donna wasn't my blood relation. She was my girlfriend and I loved her. I think that when I told her my story that was the same thing my mother done. It kept her warm right up to the time she stepped into the next world in them Charles Jordan shoes. That's why she died with a smile on her face.

Like I said, I would of burned her things after four days if her son hadn't turned up like that and kicked me out of her place. I need to make a fire for Donna, and one for me too. I thought I might as well burn this story like my picture book, but I haven't

122

decided about that yet. Maybe I'll send it to my white mother. She is a writer too, now that her kids are grown up.

Some guys can make magic. I seen them on TV. They can pull rabbits out of hats. Some of them TV preachers can make crippled people get out of wheelchairs. I seen a shaman make sick people better too. I never had that kind of power. When I was a kid, I always had a box of matches in my pocket. And then April gave me a magnifying glass for looking at things up close. Mitchell showed me how to catch the sun with it. That was the only magic I could do.

I liked lighting the dry grass on fire. It burned so beautiful. You didn't need sticks, or gas, or paper, or nothing like that. The only scary time was when you couldn't stop it. I liked stopping the fires too.

I got better at fires all the time. Every one was better than the last. It was too bad I only made a little fire at Father's house. I was scared to go back and burn the place down, but I did get a whole church once. It wasn't Father's church. It was the little one by the river. That was a good fire. It was like them burning schoolhouses we had at the farm on Hallowe'en.

My best fire ever was the hairdressers'. It had such great colours. I bet my mother in heaven saw that one. I wanted her to see me and bend down and say my names loud enough so everyone could hear my real father's name and the Indian name I never got because both my parents went to spirit so soon.

I seen my real father's house burn down on TV. That was the number one fire I ever saw. I wish I was the guy to start it. Somebody else got to do that, maybe another kid that he got from seeing his mother dance around the fire in a far away place.

Pret'soon I'm going to see my real father and he is going to see me. I'm gonna catch a ride to Mount Garibaldi with some Indians who live up that way. Maybe me and my dad will sit around the fire in his cabin on the sacred mountain and eat food together. We will look in the fire and I will say his name and he will say mine. That will be a good day.

33.
Snow

When the doctor told Donna that first time in the hospital, she said the room turned white. It was like it was full of snow and she couldn't hear nothing. She said she was scared. I said now you know how an Indian feels when he walks into a room full of white people. Me and Donna both had a sickness and it was being afraid of what was gonna happen next. I said don't be afraid. I will take care of you, and I did, eh? I did the best I could and the China White carrying her off like a snow angel.

I love snow the best. That is when the whole world looks like a queen in a fur coat. I seen my mother like that, the night she died. I still see her. My mother is very still. Snow comes in the car window and lands on her black hairs and her cheeks and shoulders and stays cold. It never melts. She comes in my dreams like that all the time. In my dreams, she is smiling. She floats out of the car window and up into the night where all the stars are shining. She could be one of those holy statues hanging in the air.

I got to think of something and hold on to it. I already seen

M'zelle go by in a gold car with the top down, her hair as hot as the sun. I seen Donna dancing in some sparkly heaven shoes. I seen a field of them white lilies come up through the snow and shake out their green leaves all in the time it took for him to ski from the top to the bottom of the mountain. I heard them lilies sing like the song April learned me and the other kids. I hope Starlene has told it to our daughter along with the Indian songs they learned her in the Bighouse when she got grabbed.

I hear all them spirits, ours and theirs, even though they are invisible like me. Only it don't matter no more. There is no next to be afraid of. Now I see my mother and that is all. She is reaching her arms down and they are covered with snow.

I am covered with snow. My arms are heavy and cold. My throat is almost empty. I been beating my drum and saying my name all day, and now it is night. The ghosts are coming out of the trees. They are all the children that went to spirit since I came here to finish what started that night my mother got born again in the snow.

The children are cold. They are carrying branches. I am going to make a fire for all of us. It will start with my dress. I will light fire to my dress and the children will light their branches. They will take their burning branches back to the trees. The birds will rise up, singing like spirits, and so will the children. I will sing as long as I can.

Today I seen him and he seen me. The whole mountain will burn and he will feel the heat of it on his back when he walks away. It will be a beautiful fire.

MEMBER OF THE SCABRINI GROUP

Quebec, Canada
2000